SHERRYL WOODS has published fifty novels since 1982 and has sold over five million books worldwide. She has written seven books in the highly acclaimed Amanda Roberts mystery series. A former news reporter in the South, very much like her highly praised fictional sleuth Amanda Roberts, Sherryl Woods now divides her time between Los Angeles and Key Biscayne, Florida.

Sherryl Woods

Deadly Obsession

WARNER BOOKS

A Time Warner Company

WARNER BOOKS EDITION

Copyright © 1995 by Sherryl Woods
All rights reserved.

Cover design by Jacki Merri Meyer
Cover photograph by Herman Estevez

Warner Books, Inc.
1271 Avenue of the Americas
New York, NY 10020

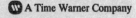 A Time Warner Company

Printed in the United States of America

First Printing: May, 1995

10 9 8 7 6 5 4 3 2 1

CHAPTER

One

Postpartum depression. Some women got it after delivering babies. Journalist Amanda Roberts got it after turning in stories. The minute she had delivered her last exposé to *Inside Atlanta* magazine, she wondered if five minutes of euphoria over solving the puzzle was worth this awful *what-next* sensation that always occurred immediately afterward. She wished the high would last until the article was in print at least. Now she also had to contend with the worrisome glint of anticipation in the eyes of editor Oscar Cates, who was always thinking ahead to the magazine's next edition.

Just this morning Oscar had suggested that if Amanda didn't come up with a fascinating story idea soon, he'd offer one of his own. She almost always hated Oscar's ideas. Since the November issue was coming up, he'd probably ship her off to some farm to do a feature on turkeys or, worse yet, to some socialite's home for a photo layout on setting a decorative Thanksgiving table in the Southern tradition.

In an act of desperation she began cleaning out files, hoping that some slip of paper would trigger an idea for her next investigative piece for the magazine. Unfortunately, she could spend weeks sorting through notes written on napkins and the backs of grocery store receipts without finding anything more exciting than a scribbled phone number for some no longer identifiable source.

She was reaching for her just-filled jar of gourmet Jelly Belly jelly beans, hoping that maybe a burst of tangerine would put a little zest into her mood, when a shadow fell over her desk. Fortunately, it was a tall, lean shadow. Definitely not the ever-dieting Oscar, she decided. She dared a glance up.

"Ms. Roberts?"

She nodded, studying the man, who appeared to be in his mid-thirties and who was eyeing her jeans and T-shirt with a disapproving scowl. He had the look of a man intent on ferreting out Atlanta's worst-dressed professionals. Unfortunately, Amanda's designer-clad mother would have agreed with his quick assessment of her daughter. Amanda's casual, but practical look would never make her a candidate for a fashion award.

Certainly this guy's attire would have withstood any designer's test. From his perfectly tailored gray suit, pristine white silk blend shirt with monogrammed cuffs and heavy gold cuff links, right down to his expensive, polished shoes, he was a testament to money and taste. Amanda couldn't imagine how people got through an entire day without a single scuff mark on their shoes. Maybe it required an attentive valet residing in the back of the limo. She glanced down at her own dull loafers and hurriedly tucked her feet out of sight under the desk. Since she couldn't crawl after them, she lifted her chin and met her visitor's gaze head-on.

"Can I help you?" she asked politely, though she wasn't

particularly inclined to be helpful to someone whose chiseled, aristocratic features betrayed such a haughty, supercilious attitude.

"I understand that you have quite a reputation as an investigative reporter," he said.

He made the observation with an expression of distaste that suggested he considered reporters only one step above pond scum on the evolutionary ladder. It also sounded as if he had no firsthand knowledge of a single word she had written. If he'd hoped to flatter her, he was off to a bad start. Amanda was beginning to grind her teeth.

"So they say," she responded noncommittally.

He glanced pointedly at the chair beside her desk. "May I sit?"

"Be my guest."

When his jacket was neatly straightened and his cuffs precisely adjusted, he announced, "I am Hamilton Kenilworth."

He paused as if that were supposed to draw *ohhs* and *ahhs*. Amanda had never heard of him. She tried her best, however, to look as if she had and as if she were duly impressed. "I see."

"Of Kenilworth, Kenilworth, James and Donovan."

"Of course." She still didn't have a clue about who he was, but whenever names were strung together that way and spoken about with such reverence, she had to assume it was a law firm. She made a point of knowing as few lawyers as possible. Looking longingly at her jar of jelly beans, she wished she could politely scoop out a handful and find the soothing ice-blue mint-flavored ones. She had a feeling this was not going to be a pleasant encounter.

"This is a rather delicate matter," Mr. Hamilton Kenilworth said eventually.

"I see," she said, though to be perfectly honest she didn't understand why this man had deigned to pay her a visit when it was evident he didn't consider her to be in his social or professional league.

"May I count on your discretion?" he asked, regarding her intently.

Discretion? The word sparked a certain amount of hope. It usually implied deep, dark secrets. Maybe whatever he had to say would lead to something more exciting than a feature on turkey sightings or the making of little Pilgrim people from corn husks.

"Mr. Kenilworth, I suppose I am as discreet as the next person," she said. "But you must understand that generally people who come to me expect me to print something in a widely circulated regional magazine. Professionally speaking, I am not in the business of keeping secrets."

He colored a bit at that, an amazing reaction from someone she'd already decided was bloodless.

"Of course," he said. "It's just that this isn't something I'm in the habit of doing."

"You mean talking to a reporter," she guessed.

He drew himself up until he was sitting ramrod stiff. Some private school deportment teacher would have been proud of that posture. Amanda thought he looked downright uncomfortable. He also didn't seem inclined to elaborate.

Amanda decided this had to be some kind of diabolical test, perhaps dreamed up by Oscar to see how long it would be before she exploded impatiently and begged to do some lousy Thanksgiving feature. She figured—at the outside—it would take another five minutes of this awkward conversation.

Kenilworth's gaze met hers, then shifted away. "Actually, I meant baring my soul."

Clearly that explained why he didn't have much knack for it, she decided. "To a stranger?" she asked.

"To anyone."

Now, that Amanda could believe. Hamilton Kenilworth did not strike her as the sort of man who was actually in touch with his feelings, assuming he had any under that spit-and-polish exterior. She looked into his eyes, expecting to see little emotion in the cool, gray depths. Instead, his eyes were the slate gray of a stormy sea. Her level of interest increased another notch or two. She loved discovering seething passion under a calm exterior. It usually meant she was one step away from the heart of a story.

"Could I get you a cup of coffee?" she offered, hoping that would relax him so he'd spill his guts in a more timely fashion.

He shook his head. "No, really, I think it's best if I just get this over with. You see, it's about my child, Lauren. And my wife, of course," he added almost as an afterthought.

His gaze met Amanda's and this time there was no mistaking the turmoil. "They're missing."

He said it with a bleak matter-of-factness that sent a chill down her spine. "Have you contacted the police?"

"No."

"Why not?"

"Believe me, I know how the police will regard this. You see, it's not the first time Margaret has disappeared. She gets some crazy idea into her head and just takes off, dragging Lauren with her. In the past, though, she's always come back, just about the time she figures I'll be frantic. That's why the police won't take it seriously. They've seen what's happened on the previous occasions."

Amanda wondered whether she dared to suggest counseling. It seemed more appropriate than bringing his tale of marital woes to a reporter. The last thing she wanted to get involved in was some convoluted domestic dispute. The news value, outside of some tabloid's circulation, was minimal. Amanda prayed daily that *Inside Atlanta* would remain above printing sleaze. Though Oscar had clearly had his temptations to overcome, thus far her prayers had been answered.

"Have you considered hiring a private detective?"

"I've had one working on the case for the past week. He has come up with nothing, not a single trace. She hasn't turned up in any of the usual places. She's not with her family. She hasn't gone to our beach house in Hilton Head. Her best friend hasn't spoken with her in over two weeks. Frankly, I'm getting worried that something has happened this time. That's why I'm turning to you."

Amanda still wasn't entirely clear about where she fit into his plans and she was sure he had very definite plans in mind. His kind of pin-striped, button-down types always did. "I'm a reporter, Mr. Kenilworth. Not a detective. Where's the story?"

He regarded her with a wry expression. "Prominent attorney's wife flees with his daughter. What sort of scandal drove her away? Where is she hiding?" He dropped the tabloid tenor from his manner and said in a smug tone that was more in character, "I can't imagine that the questions wouldn't intrigue you."

"Let me get this straight. You want me to find your wife and daughter, and out of this I get what?"

"A story that will sell magazines, of course. The Kenilworth name on the cover ought to do it. If that won't, the Clayton name will. Margaret is a Clayton."

Amanda had never heard of the Claytons. But to her regret, she could definitely see the possibilities, especially if Kenilworth, Kenilworth, James and Donovan carried the kind of social clout he seemed to think it did. Visions of an insider view of Georgia's old-boys network danced in her head. She wished she could slip away to confirm Kenilworth's claim with Oscar, who could trace most Georgia family trees back to their roots. She knew, however, that now was not a good time to interrupt a man baring his soul for the first time. He was liable to think better of it and split.

She had to admit she was fascinated, if also a little outraged, by people who used their children as pawns in domestic quarrels. Certainly a story such as this would give her an opportunity to explore that issue, maybe talk to some psychologists about the impact on the young victims of such adult power struggles. That would be a spin she could live with.

And right now, with a mysterious teenage runaway living in her own home, she was already caught up in one dysfunctional family drama on a very personal level. Exploring the Kenilworths' troubles as she delved into Pete's background seemed like a way to weave the usually diverse threads of her life into a single strand for a change.

Still, she didn't much like Hamilton Kenilworth. Something told her that Mrs. Kenilworth had been one smart cookie to get herself far away from the smug bastard. Gut instinct made her disinclined to help him in any way. For once in her life, she wasn't overcome by a need to meddle in other people's lives, even from a safe journalistic distance.

"Why would you want to air your family problems like this?" she asked. Somehow it just didn't fit with his uptight image.

"The more people I have looking for them, the sooner I will have my daughter back with me. And my wife, of course," he added, again almost as an afterthought.

Amanda's gut instincts also told her there was something more going on than what Hamilton Kenilworth was telling her. Something also warned her that she didn't want to know what it was.

"I'm sorry. I don't think so," she said finally. "I think you'd be better off leaving this in the hands of your detective."

He looked momentarily surprised, then more determined and grim-faced than ever. "Just think about it," he urged. "Promise me you will take the night and think it over. It's possible, Ms. Roberts, that a child's future is at stake."

"Are you saying that your wife is an unfit mother?"

He avoided her scrutiny. "That would be something you'd have to explore, wouldn't it?"

"Mr. Kenilworth, I'm really not interested in sitting here playing word games with you," she snapped impatiently. "Is your child in some sort of danger or not?"

"If I tell you that she is, will you do the story?"

"No, I'll call the police."

He gave a nod of satisfaction. "Good. That is what I would expect you to say. As I anticipated, you'll do quite nicely."

Amanda bristled at the suggestion that he'd been testing her ethics in some way. "Mr. Kenilworth, you're not interviewing me to play nanny to your child. You're asking me to launch a full-scale investigation into her whereabouts, to dissect your family life for some clue that will lead me to her and to your wife. Are you aware that such scrutiny won't be pleasant and that when I'm finished, all the messy details will be made public?"

"Ms. Roberts, I just want my child back," he said quietly. "I'll pay whatever personal price that requires. If my wife is embarrassed, well, then, she should have thought of that before leaving, shouldn't she?"

He reached in his pocket and pulled out a photograph. For several minutes, he studied it, then sighed and laid it on Amanda's desk, along with a business card. "I will expect your answer in the morning."

He stood then and walked away without a backward glance. Amanda glared after him. The lousy, self-satisfied son-of-a-bitch, she thought indignantly.

Finally, when she could stand it no longer, she picked up the snapshot. Gray eyes stared back at her from a cherubic face framed by a halo of golden curls. The child looked to be five, maybe six years old, and was obviously dressed for a special occasion in her elaborately smocked pale blue dress and patent leather shoes, the kind of outfit that cost major bucks in some fancy kids' boutique. Her far too serious expression struck a responsive chord deep inside Amanda. She immediately wanted to see smudges of dirt on the child's cheeks and laughter in those solemn eyes.

The real killer, though, was the expression on the face of the man holding her in the photograph. The cool, distant demeanor that Amanda had found so irritating in Hamilton Kenilworth just now was the antithesis of the warmth and adoration on his face as he gazed at the daughter he held. She had pegged the lawyer as someone who loved only three things—money, power, and position. Now, faced with the evidence in this one snapshot, Amanda was forced to revise her opinion. Hamilton Kenilworth also loved his daughter, maybe even above everything else.

"Well, hell," Amanda muttered at the discovery. She supposed she was going to investigate his story after all.

She realized the lawyer had guessed she would do exactly that when he deliberately left that photograph on her desk. She couldn't deny feeling manipulated. But she also couldn't deny the flare of excitement that overtook her every time she began to dig into a new story. Disconcerting, though, was the unexpected hint of dread that this time she wasn't going to like what she uncovered one little bit.

C H A P T E R

TWO

*H*amilton Kenilworth, as it turned out, was not exactly the publicity-shy creature Amanda had guessed him to be. Her search through computerized data revealed dozens of articles about high-profile legal cases he'd won, along with several features on the family, which had apparently dominated Atlanta social circles since the dawn of time. If it weren't for the currently messy separation he'd revealed to her, she would have surmised he was gearing up to run for political office.

One thing puzzled her, though. With all of these mostly favorable prior media contacts to turn to, why had he come to her with this particular story? Perhaps he'd assumed she would be less biased. Perhaps because she alone in all of Atlanta wasn't already hip deep in Kenilworth lore. Perhaps because she was the last journalist in all of Georgia for him to conquer. Who could figure what made a man like Hamilton Kenilworth tick?

A magna cum laude graduate of the Yale Law School, as his

father and grandfather had been before him, he had followed a career path that was already paved in gold. The oldest, most prominent Atlanta families turned to Kenilworth, Kenilworth, James and Donovan for their most private peccadilloes and their most public scandals.

When heiress Melanie Louise Grayson had sued her second husband, Buddy, for divorce after catching him in bed with the upstairs maid, Hamilton Kenilworth I, had settled the whole matter over drinks one afternoon at the country club. The society columnists in town had practically wept over the speed and discretion with which it had all been resolved. Melanie had kept the house, her fortune, and her jewels. Buddy had walked away with the clothes on his back, a payoff, and a threat to keep the details to himself or risk losing that reportedly generous settlement.

And when Willie Townsend of the Buckhead Townsends had blown away his gay lover in a fit of jealous rage, Hamilton Kenilworth II had handled the distasteful mess with a brilliant defense that had brought jurors to tears.

Yes, indeed, Amanda thought, the Kenilworths—father and son—were definitely the attorneys of choice for a certain social set. Such skilled defenders, however, ought to have had an entire army of excellent private investigators at their command. Once again, she had to wonder why Hamilton Kenilworth had brought his sad tale to her, knowing that it was going to end up in print. Was he more interested in finding Lauren or in getting even with his wandering wife? It was the kind of question that made her very edgy. It suggested that she was being duped big-time.

Amanda's hackles rose at the possibility that Kenilworth thought he could manipulate her. Just to test her theory that that was what he had in mind, she wandered into Oscar's office. Shoving aside a pile of printouts, she perched on the corner of his desk and waited for him to look up from his computer screen.

"You ever heard of chairs?" he grumbled without glancing up.

Amanda directed a pointed look at the three chairs currently buried beneath stacks of debris, some of which might actually have been important. She doubted anyone would ever know, if it was left up to Oscar to sort through it.

"You ever heard of filing?" she countered.

He scowled at her. "Did you have a reason for coming in here other than hassling me?"

"Oh, I thought I'd mention the story I'm working on, see if you had any insights you'd care to offer."

That finally got his full attention. "Since when do you ask me anything?" he inquired suspiciously and with a certain amount of justification.

"Since a major-league lawyer came tripping up to my desk earlier to suggest I might want to help him find his missing wife and daughter."

"What lawyer?"

When Amanda told him, Oscar leaned back in his chair and whistled. "So what's the deal? Is he on the level? Has he reported this to the police?"

"He says the police won't take it seriously, because his wife does this all the time."

Oscar's expression turned sour. "Then it's not news. Tell him to hire a private detective."

"I did."

"And?"

"He has, but he seems to want his dirty laundry aired in print as well."

"I don't get it."

"Frankly, neither do I."

"Then why the hell are you talking to me about this? You're not shy. Tell him no and get to work on something else. I told you this morning, I have some great ideas for Thanksgiving."

Amanda shuddered. "I told him no. Then he showed me this." She tossed the photo onto Oscar's desk. She watched his expression soften. "Changes things, doesn't it?"

"Dammit, Amanda, what's your angle here?" he asked.

He'd ignored her question and fallen into the devil's advocate role she'd counted on. "Dysfunctional families using their kids as pawns. Whatever's going on between Kenilworth and his wife, does that child look as if she deserves to be caught in the middle?"

"She's one kid, Amanda."

"There are more out there, and you know it. Lauren Kenilworth's story could make people see what they're doing to their children."

Her boss sighed heavily. "If you'd already decided you were going to do this, why'd you bother asking me?"

She shrugged. "I don't know. I guess I wanted your blessing. Maybe I wanted you to tell me I can trust Hamilton Kenilworth. Maybe I wanted you to tell me to drop this before I uncover something that's going to make me sick to my stomach."

"Was that multiple choice, or did you want me to address all three? You want my blessing, you have it. You want my gut instinct about Kenilworth, don't trust him worth spit. You want me to tell you to drop the whole thing?" He shrugged and looked at the snapshot again. His shoulders slumped and his eyes turned sad. "What would be the point? In all the years you and I have worked together, you've never given a damn about my objections. I'm not about to waste my breath again."

Oscar gave her what passed for an encouraging grin. "Besides, if I had a kid missing, I can't imagine anyone better than you to get her back. You've got the grit to tell that daddy of hers to take a flying leap, if he gets in your way. Something tells me Kenilworth wasn't counting on that. Ought to make things downright interesting, don't you think?"

Interesting wasn't the word Amanda would have chosen. Tucking the snapshot into her two-year-old misshapen purse from a discount store, which no one in Kenilworth's set would be caught dead carrying, Amanda reluctantly headed out of the office in search of a more complete picture of the family whose privacy she was about to invade. On her way, she ran into Jenny Lee Macon as Jenny Lee was about to exit the elevator a full hour ahead of her scheduled start time.

Several years younger and every bit as ambitious as Amanda had been at her age, Jenny Lee had inched her way one rung up the three-step career ladder at *Inside Atlanta*. On the masthead she was officially listed as editorial assistant, the only one the magazine had. The pay was about on a par with what she'd earned as receptionist. However, the opportunities for getting into trouble were significantly improved, especially since she was teamed with Amanda. Jenny Lee apparently figured that was a better benefit than a pay raise.

"Where are you going?" she asked.

"I'm doing a little preliminary investigating into a story I might tackle." Amanda had to smother a laugh at Jenny Lee's immediately eager expression. "Okay, you can come, too."

On the way to the garage, Jenny Lee plied her with questions. At the mention of Hamilton Kenilworth, her reaction was much like Oscar's.

"You know him?" Amanda asked.

"Just what I read in the papers. You know his wife."

Amanda tried to recall Margaret Kenilworth and came up blank. "I do?"

"She used to work out at Weights and Measures. I know you've probably blocked the memory, given how you feel about exercise and all, but that was that health club where you did the story a couple of years ago."

Amanda recalled the story vividly. She still had no recollection of Mrs. Kenilworth. "Tell me about her."

"Frankly, I thought she looked anorexic. She was probably beautiful ten, fifteen years ago. She had masses and masses of gorgeous chestnut hair streaked with blond, really classic features. But at the gym she looked like she'd whittled every last ounce of fat from her body."

"Model-thin," Amanda suggested with a trace of envy. She figured she'd probably erased any memory of a woman who looked that good from her mind.

Jenny Lee shook her head. "No, thinner. It wasn't attractive. Maybe when she was all dolled up in her size-two designer dresses, she looked terrific, but in a leotard she looked gaunt. Her legs were the size of itty-bitty twigs. Her face looked almost haggard. I felt kinda sorry for her. I kept wanting to feed her lots of grits and redeye gravy or lots of fried chicken and mashed potatoes."

"Did you ever talk to her?"

"Nope. She was always working out like crazy, either on the weights or taking an aerobics class."

"That place seems a little out of her neighborhood. I wonder what she was doing there."

"If she was as compulsive about working out as she seemed to me, she probably didn't want any of her friends to guess.

She probably played tennis with them all morning, then did an aerobics class at the club, then headed north for one last session before going home to dear old Hamilton."

Amanda shuddered at the very idea of all that exercise. Jenny Lee was right about her aversion to sweating. She jogged, but she was hardly fanatical about it. As for food, she ate whenever and whatever she wanted and hoped for the best. She was well aware, though, that the world was filled with women whose waist measurement was higher than their caloric intake. Quite a few of them had probably been driven to such extremes by troubled marriages.

Leaving the parking garage, she consulted her map one more time, then headed north to Buckhead, where it was rumored in those articles she'd read that the Kenilworth family mansion could have doubled for Tara in *Gone With the Wind*. At this time of day, she was hoping to find a chatty housekeeper around who'd spill the beans on the Kenilworths' family life.

Unfortunately, the dour-faced woman who opened the door of the white-columned family mansion looked as if she'd served on the staff at some haunted villa in a gothic novel. Black eyes, as cold as a granite cemetery marker, regarded Amanda with suspicion. Her uniform-clad body was thin as a rail, but she'd positioned herself in a way that denied entrance. It was not exactly the welcome Amanda had been hoping for.

"I'd like to see Mrs. Kenilworth, please," Amanda said, assuming her most uncharacteristically demure demeanor. The strain of it was going to tell if she had to keep it up for long.

"Who are you?"

"I'm Amanda Roberts. This is Jenny Lee Macon." Amanda beamed at her, then seized on the information Jenny Lee had given her. "We know Mrs. Kenilworth from the gym."

The icy demeanor didn't defrost so much as a degree. "She's not here."

"We wouldn't mind waiting," Amanda said. "Would we, Jenny Lee?"

"We surely wouldn't," Jenny Lee chimed in, affecting her very best Southern drawl as if that might counteract the suspiciousness of Amanda's New York accent. "I'm sure she told us to be here just before noon. Isn't that right, Amanda, honey?"

"That's right. We were going to the club for lunch."

The housekeeper might have believed them or she might not. There was no way to tell. She folded her arms across her middle. "She must have forgot. I'm not expecting her back by noon."

"Oh, dear," Jenny Lee murmured. "We must have gotten our dates crossed. Would you mind if I used the phone for just a second to call the country club and check to make sure they have a reservation?"

Judging by the housekeeper's expression, good manners were at war with a strong desire to be rid of them. "I suppose that would be okay," she finally conceded with obvious reluctance. Fortunately, she didn't seem to be aware that every woman in Margaret's social set would probably have a cellular phone in her purse.

She led the way through the amazingly elaborate foyer with its crystal chandelier, ornate gold-framed mirrors, and Aubusson carpet to a small sitting room overlooking a garden. She gestured to the phone sitting on a small Queen Anne desk, then took up her guard position at the door. Her presence severely limited Amanda's ability to explore.

While Jenny Lee faked her call to the club, Amanda did

her best to survey the room for signs of recent habitation. Unfortunately, there was no tossed-aside newspaper to indicate the last date anyone had been present. Nor was there a stack of dated correspondence waiting to be signed and mailed. There wasn't even an opened book to suggest that someone had just left off reading it in the middle. Hell, there wasn't even a speck of dust on the surface of the gleaming antique furniture. The room was so tidy and impersonal it might have been unused for years.

The only hint that a family actually lived there was a portrait above the mantel. The massive oil painting had been done when Lauren was probably two or three. She was sitting on her daddy's knee in another one of those costly, too-precious outfits. The artist had captured the child's solemn expression as well as her father's obvious adoration. He'd been less successful with Margaret. She looked blank, as if she'd retreated to some other place far from the husband and child seated next to her. That total lack of expression was a sad counterpoint to her glowing satin gown and the brilliant jewels which shimmered with vibrant life at her throat.

While Jenny Lee wrapped up her conversation, Amanda turned back to the housekeeper and tried one last time to pry information from her. "I don't suppose you have any idea where I might reach Mrs. Kenilworth, so we can reschedule? We really would like to get together with her later this afternoon, if she's available. Perhaps she keeps a calendar in her desk?"

"She doesn't. Carries it with her," the woman said with an air of triumph, as if she'd guessed that she'd foiled Amanda's last and most inventive attempt to snoop.

"Then perhaps I can just leave her a note on the desk,"

Amanda said, already moving around Jenny Lee and reaching for a drawer handle. "There must be a pen and paper here someplace."

Pen and paper materialized in front of her faster than she could get the drawer all the way open. The housekeeper slid the drawer back into place with a brisk motion. "Always keep a pad of paper in my pocket in case the missus wants to give instructions," she said.

Amanda managed a weak smile. "How efficient," she praised. "Thank you." She scribbled a hopefully illegible note that wouldn't betray her presence in the house to Hamilton Kenilworth and tucked it into a corner of the leather-edged desk blotter. With any luck, the eagle-eyed housekeeper would forget her name and no one would be the wiser about this totally unproductive visit.

Not until they were back outside and in the car did Amanda dare a look at Jenny Lee.

"Did you feel like you were in the middle of *Wuthering Heights* or something?" Jenny Lee asked, giving an exaggerated shiver.

"Other than confirming that Margaret Kenilworth is definitely absent at this moment, I just felt like we were wasting our time."

"Not such a waste," Jenny Lee countered. "Obviously you didn't notice that little stack of unopened letters or invitations or whatever they were on the corner of the desk. I managed to mess up the pile so I could get a look at the postmarks. The one on top was dated day before yesterday, so it could have been in today's mail. The one on the bottom, though, was dated nearly a month ago."

Amanda sighed. "Which just about confirms that Margaret Kenilworth doesn't open her mail."

"Or," Jenny Lee corrected, "she's been missing for even longer than her husband told you."

"Possible," Amanda said slowly. But why, when he'd been so forthcoming about everything else, would Hamilton Kenilworth have chosen to lie about a detail like that?

C H A P T E R

Three

I f the Kenilworth home was a twin to Tara, then the house where Margaret's parents lived was the equivalent in size, if not architecture, to Buckingham Palace. From the street, hidden as it mostly was by gigantic oaks and dogwoods, it seemed merely impressive. As Amanda wound her way up the curving drive, the house emerged from the heavily wooded estate in palatial splendor.

"Holy shit," she murmured. "Looks as if old Margaret married down, not up. Who would've guessed?"

She glanced at Jenny Lee and caught the amusement in her eyes. "You guessed," she accused.

"I don't know anyone born in the whole state of Georgia who doesn't know about the Claytons," Jenny Lee responded. "They swept in here as carpetbaggers after the war—"

"Which war would that be?" Amanda asked.

Jenny Lee frowned at her. "The War Between the States," she said as if no other war could possibly have mattered. "Anyway, it was a hundred or so years ago when they barged in, bought up a lot of land, and got their fingers into as many pies as they could. They may have more money than the Kenilworths, but they're still outsiders, so don't you go thinking that Hamilton got the better of the deal. There's folks around these parts who still think he married beneath him. Pedigree counts for more than money in those circles. Damn Yankees, even a few generations removed, need not apply. I'd say there are still a handful of homes in this town where the Claytons are not welcomed and Hamilton is regarded as a traitor."

"Unbelievable," Amanda said. She could hardly wait to meet the wealthy outcasts.

Margaret Clayton Kenilworth's mother greeted them at the front door, which immediately disarmed Amanda, who'd been expecting another forbidding housekeeper or maybe even an uptight butler. She hadn't expected this fragile, fading flower of a woman. Lauralee Clayton was apparently yet another attempt on the part of the Claytons to marry into Southern tradition. She had a syrupy accent, a delicate face, and the bearing of a graduate of Miss Ella Mae's School of Deportment and Social Graces. A genuine steel magnolia.

Amanda introduced herself and Jenny Lee. Then, because she wasn't up to another session of subterfuge, she admitted candidly that she was looking into Margaret's disappearance. Mrs. Clayton seemed inclined to slam the door in their faces, but good breeding kept her from acting on the impulse. Instead, she drew herself up until her posture was rigid, her expression thoroughly forbidding.

"Where would you get an idea that Margaret is missing?"

"From her husband," Amanda said.

Mrs. Clayton's expression faltered. "Hamilton spoke to you? Why on earth would he do that?"

"He seems to think publicity might help him to locate your daughter."

The older woman's response to that was anything but lady-like. Amanda wasn't sure she'd heard her correctly.

"Excuse me," she said, hoping for a replay.

Mrs. Clayton did not repeat the comment, but she did open the door to admit Amanda and Jenny Lee. Her expression was grim as she led them into a room that couldn't be classified as anything other than an old-fashioned ladies' parlor. There were chintz slipcovers on the sofa and chairs, billowing sheer curtains, buckets of huge potted ferns in front of each floor-to-ceiling window, and a silver tea service on the coffee table that would have been the envy of the Queen of England.

"I think you'd better tell me exactly what that son-in-law of mine told you," Mrs. Clayton commanded.

As she spoke, she poured a good, strong Earl Gray into delicate bone china cups. A plate of tea sandwiches, crusts neatly trimmed, appeared just as magically. Amanda wondered if they kept the tray prepared and replenished around the clock on the off chance that guests might drop by.

Amanda figured this was one of those times when she was going to have to trade information. That didn't mean she had to reveal every last detail of her conversation with Kenilworth. "He said there had been some sort of problem and that Margaret left and took their daughter with her," she summarized.

Mrs. Clayton's lips tightened, as if she were trying to hold back any display of temper, but she remained staunchly silent.

"He said this has happened before," Amanda continued when it appeared that the amount of information she'd doled out wasn't going to net any sharing of new insights.

"Why?" Mrs. Clayton asked suspiciously.

"Why," Amanda repeated.

"Why would he tell you anything?" Mrs. Clayton said impatiently. "Why would he risk tarnishing that precious reputation of his? He has to know that what you're going to turn up won't be pretty."

The last was said softly, almost as if Mrs. Clayton were speculating to herself, unaware that she was fueling Amanda's curiosity.

"I gather he and your daughter have had problems for some time," Amanda prodded, hoping they were about to get somewhere.

Mrs. Clayton lifted one delicate brow. "You could say that," she said enigmatically, then seemed to come to some sort of decision.

"I suppose there's no point in beating around the bush, since you already have *his* side of things," she said with an unmistakable trace of anger. She carefully set her teacup back in its saucer, then looked Amanda directly in the eyes.

"I believe the problems started the day they met," she began. "Why Margaret was so insistent on marrying Hamilton is beyond me. Oh, Lord knows, he was handsome. Still cuts a fine figure, for that matter. And he's certainly a brilliant attorney. He's accepted in places where the Claytons are not. But the truth of it is he also has very rigid ideas about what he expects from his wife."

"Rigid? Do you mean old-fashioned?" Amanda asked.

"Antiquated is more like it. He was looking for a proper Southern hostess, a stay-at-home mother, a committee woman who would chair charity balls and keep his name on the tips of everyone's tongues. That way whenever legal disaster struck, as it inevitably does among the high and mighty, they would call him first."

"You didn't think your daughter was suited for that role?"

She laughed at that. "Margaret took after me. I dared to marry into this family of upstarts, you see. Margaret was much the same way, a free spirit, hardly the kind of traditional Southern belle who would pass her days dabbing at watercolors or organizing fund-raisers. She was more likely to be picketing city hall. She tried, though. She really did. If you ask me, the strain of it was killing her. She looked almost haunted the last time I saw her, and she was so thin a strong wind would have picked her up and carried her away. It nearly broke my heart to see all the spirit sapped right out of her."

"When was that?" Jenny Lee asked.

"About three weeks ago, maybe a little more. She brought Lauren by for tea after school." She gestured toward the tray in front of them. "Lauren loved these little sandwiches, and the cook always made pretty petit fours for her with glazed pastel icing. We started having tea parties when she was just a little thing. She would bring all her dolls and sip Kool-Aid from these fancy cups so she could be just like her grandmama."

"That was the last time you saw either of them?"

She nodded as tears welled up in her eyes. She dabbed at them with a lace-edged hankie with an embroidered monogram. The scrap of cloth released the scent of lily of the valley in the air.

"Have you spoken with Lauren's school? Did Margaret let them know she wouldn't be there for a while?" Amanda asked.

"As a matter of fact, the school called here when Lauren didn't turn up for classes. Apparently Hamilton's response hadn't been satisfactory. I've known the headmistress for years, ever since Margaret attended the same school. She was quite worried about Lauren's repeated, unexplained absences. She feels they're disruptive to the other students. She also

26

said Lauren was falling behind in her lessons and that if the situation didn't improve, they might not be able to accept Lauren for the second semester. I pleaded with her to be patient and I think I was able to convince her, but this has to be the last time Margaret does something like this. I could hear that in Mrs. Longworth's voice. She was quite put out."

"Do you have any idea at all where Margaret might have gone?" Amanda asked. "Mr. Kenilworth mentioned a home in Hilton Head."

"My husband drove down there and looked for her. The house was closed up tight. She hadn't been seen by any of the neighbors."

"And her best friend? He mentioned that she hasn't heard from Margaret either."

"That would be Charlotte Anne Donovan," Mrs. Clayton explained. "She's married to one of the partners in the law firm, Gil Donovan. Lottie and Margaret went all through school together, starting back in kindergarten at Mrs. Longworth's Academy. In the past, it's true, Margaret has gone to Lottie when she felt the need to hide away for a bit."

"Why not come here?"

Mrs. Clayton's lips thinned again. "Because my husband, who is in most instances a wise and decent man, has very strong beliefs on the subject. Truth be told, he's more old-fashioned and Southern than I am, despite where his great-granddaddy came from. He feels that a woman shouldn't run out on her husband under any circumstances. He'd just insist she go back home and settle her problems. So Margaret would turn to Lottie, where she could be sure there would be acceptance."

Amanda was beginning to get a faint inkling that the unmentioned circumstances related to abuse. There was no way to phrase the question delicately. She had to be blunt. "Mrs. Clayton, was your daughter being abused by her husband?"

"Oh, dear heaven, no!" The older woman looked so thoroughly horrified by the suggestion that there was no doubting that her response was the truth, at least as she knew it. "Not in the way you mean, certainly. It was just all of those rigid expectations. Only a saint could have lived up to them. Margaret isn't a saint." She sighed heavily. "Few of us are."

"Would Lottie keep Margaret's whereabouts secret, if she does know?" Amanda asked.

Mrs. Clayton looked thoughtful. "Why, yes," she said finally. "Yes, I believe she would. Her first loyalty would be to Margaret."

"Even though her husband and Margaret's are law partners?"

"That wouldn't matter to Lottie," she said confidently. "I recall when she was just a child and she was blamed for something perfectly dreadful like deliberately dumping paint on the teacher's gradebook and ruining a whole semester's records. Everyone guessed Margaret was the one really responsible, but no one was able to pry the truth out of Lottie. Margaret finally confessed to get poor Lottie off the hook."

"Do you have her address and phone number?" Amanda asked. "I'd like to speak to her anyway."

"Of course. I'll get them for you. I have them in my desk in the other room. Excuse me for just a moment. I'll send cook in with some of those petit fours I mentioned."

A silver serving plate, topped by a doily and a little mound of cakes, was deposited next to the tea service within minutes. Amanda eyed them hopefully. "Do you suppose at that size, they don't have calories?"

"At that size, they probably have twice as many calories

as what you're used to eating. It's all that butter and sugar," Jenny Lee said. "Those little devils will go straight to your hips."

Amanda ignored the warning and popped one in her mouth. It was light as air. Buttery air, that is. Moist. Sweet. Yep, it was definitely heading straight for her hips. She didn't care. She ate two more before Jenny Lee's disapproving scowl finally got to her. "You're not paid to be my conscience, you know."

Jenny Lee grinned. "I know. I do it out of the goodness of my heart."

"Save it for somebody else," Amanda advised, eying one pretty little pink cake with a swirl of mint green on the top. Only the return of Mrs. Clayton kept her from nabbing it.

"Here you are, dear." She handed over a monogrammed vellum note card with the information Amanda had requested written out neatly in a flowing script. "Lottie lives not too far from here, but I doubt you'll find her home this time of day. You might catch her at the country club, though. She's probably just finishing up her tennis game about now."

Tennis games. Luncheons. Tea cakes. How did these women survive the monotony of it? Amanda wondered as she and Jenny Lee headed toward the country club. Apparently Margaret Kenilworth hadn't. She'd repeatedly fled the social scene. Suddenly feeling sorry for the woman whose choice of a mate had forced her into an ill-fitting niche, Amanda's determination to find her increased.

"I recognize that look," Jenny Lee said worriedly.

"What look?"

"The look that tells me you're identifying in some weird way with Margaret Kenilworth."

"So?"

"If you find her, you're not going to tell her husband where she is, are you?"

Amanda sighed. "I guess that depends on whether or not Margaret wants him to know."

"Margaret's not the only one involved, though. There's Lauren, too," Jenny Lee pointed out. "She's the one who got you fascinated with this story to begin with. Don't forget that right now she's separated from a daddy she probably adores."

No," Amanda corrected thoughtfully. "We know Hamilton adores her." She drew the snapshot out of her purse and examined it again. "Look at this. Look at how sad she looks. She looked the same way in the portrait in that sitting room we were in at their house."

"Maybe she just doesn't like to sit still," Jenny Lee countered. "My sister doesn't have one decent picture of her little boy. Every time she gets him near that Sears photographer, he screams his head off and squirms so much he's usually all blurry."

"You could be right, I suppose," Amanda conceded. "Or maybe she's miserable, just like her mother." Another possibility, one she didn't even want to speak aloud, crossed her mind. Jenny Lee's sharply indrawn breath suggested she might have had the same thought.

"Amanda," Jenny Lee said anxiously, "you don't suppose he's ever touched that child."

Amanda hesitated. Just talking about the possibility of child abuse made her skin crawl. "It would explain why Margaret keeps disappearing, why no one knows where she is," Amanda said. "She might have taken Lauren because she knew she could never get full custody in any kind of court where the Kenilworths are regarded with awe."

Amanda shivered. Then an image of Hamilton Kenilworth

popped into her mind. As cold and arrogant as she'd found him, she still couldn't envision him as a child molester. "Let's not get too carried away here," she cautioned.

Jenny Lee regarded her with astonishment. "Me? You jumped to the very same conclusion."

"And now I'm backing away from it. This is one time when I want every single fact laid out in front of me before I reach any conclusions at all."

"Right," Jenny Lee said skeptically.

"I mean it. Donelli's always accusing me of making snap judgments," she said, referring to her husband of less than six months. Her quick dismissal of suspects in murder investigations had just about driven the ex-Brooklyn cop nuts.

Not even Joe could deny, however, that more often than not her gut instincts had proven to be accurate. This time her gut told her that child abuse was not the problem in the Kenilworth family dynamics. Picturing that sweet, sad child, she realized she had never wanted more desperately to be proven right.

CHAPTER
Four

*T*he circular drive at the Ashlawn Country Club was lined with sporty little Mercedes and BMW convertibles, with an occasional Cadillac and LeBaron thrown in by those who were violently opposed to buying foreign. Except for its coating of dull red dust, Amanda's prized white convertible fit right in.

She wished she could say the same about her clothes. She looked like a dull wren amid a flock of parrots. She had had no idea that warm-up suits came in so many styles and colors. Nor had she been aware that diamond stud earrings and diamond tennis bracelets worth approximately as much as her annual salary were suitable accessories for them. The fact that the tennis rackets and golf clubs lined up under the porte cochere could have been pawned for enough cash to feed a small nation added to the sense of unreality.

If she weren't anxious to track down Lottie Donovan, nothing could have lured her inside this place. As it was, Jenny Lee had to prod her along.

"Nobody lives like this," she muttered under her breath with an air of disbelief. "Nobody."

"Obviously you've been part of the working world for too long," Jenny Lee corrected. "There's a whole layer of society where this is the norm. Hamilton Kenilworth is just the tip of the iceberg."

Inside the lavish lobby with its marble floors and antique tables topped by vases crammed with bouquets of fresh flowers, a uniformed man intercepted them. His demeanor was courtly enough, but there was no mistaking the *stop-here* command behind the pleasantly spoken "May I help you?"

"We're here to meet Mrs. Donovan," Amanda said matter-of-factly. She'd discovered that acting as if she belonged could whiz a reporter right past a lot of tight security.

Not this time. Though he beamed at them with an air of genteel welcome, the man subtly blocked their path. "Let me check the book."

Amanda exchanged a look with Jenny Lee, pleading for some of her fancy Southern footwork. Jenny Lee didn't disappoint her. She jumped right in, putting a delicate hand on his burly arm.

"Sugar, Mrs. Donovan's expecting us. I'm sure she's probably in the dining room starving to death. We'll be in there, okay?"

He didn't budge, didn't even glance at Jenny Lee's hand. "Afraid not. Members always leave the names of their guests with me. If they don't, the rules say I have to check. I'll make a quick call to the dining room and we can clear this right up, I'm sure. Who shall I tell Mrs. Donovan is here?"

Amanda left that answer to Jenny Lee, hoping she'd have an inspiration. Jenny Lee's verbal tap-dancing usually left even Amanda feeling a little awed. Sure enough, her assistant never hesitated.

"Jenny Lee Macon. I'm cousin to Margaret Kenilworth. I believe Margaret's a member here, too," she said, giving him her broadest smile while she surreptitiously examined his name tag. William. Apparently he was undeserving of a last name.

"We're just up from Savannah for the day, William, hon. The truth of it is, we were hoping to surprise Lottie and Margaret. You wouldn't want to spoil that, would you?"

Jenny Lee's sweet-talk was having an effect. William swallowed hard. "A surprise?"

"Yes, I swear to you, we won't get you in trouble. If anyone asks how we slipped in, we'll tell 'em you were all tied up helping a member and we just sneaked right on past. Please, sugar. Don't spoil this for dear cousin Margaret and her friend."

William, whose gray hair suggested he had probably seen and heard a lot in his time, should have been immune to such deceptive wiles. Apparently, though, he wasn't entirely immune to a pretty young woman. He winked at Jenny Lee. "I'm just going to look in the lost and found room for that coat one of the members reported missing. When I get back, you two had better be nowhere in sight."

Jenny Lee beamed at him. "Thanks, sugar."

As they sped around the corner and headed for the dining room, where it turned out that Jenny Lee had dined on more than one occasion with wealthy relatives she rarely discussed, Amanda regarded her with amusement. "Sugar? You laid it on a little thick, didn't you? The man's probably having palpitations right this second."

"We're back here and not in the parking lot on our tushes, aren't we? Don't knock my technique. You know darn good and well it works better at a place like this than yours would or you wouldn't have left it to me back there."

"Touché," Amanda replied, laughing. "It is a pleasure to watch you work, *sugar*. Now, how do you propose we find our dear friend Lottie Donovan?"

"That's a snap," Jenny Lee said airily. She snagged a waiter and five seconds later she and Amanda were crossing the dining room toward a table overlooking the gardens and a sweep of lawn that bordered the first tee of the golf course.

Charlotte Donovan—Lottie—was seated at a table for four with just one companion. How convenient, Amanda thought as they approached. Two chairs were left just for her and Jenny Lee. Startled brown eyes looked up from a menu when Amanda sat down.

"I beg your pardon," Lottie said, her perfectly shaped little nose in the air. "Who are you? These seats aren't available. If you don't leave at once, I shall have to call William."

Amanda knew all about William. She doubted even Jenny Lee could talk her way around old Willie if Mrs. Donovan made good on her threat to have them tossed out.

"Please, Mrs. Donovan, I'm Amanda Roberts from *Inside Atlanta*. This is my assistant, Jenny Lee Macon. I really need to speak with you about Margaret Kenilworth. We won't take but a minute."

An instant's doubt flickered in Mrs. Donovan's eyes. It gave Amanda hope. She glanced at the other woman. "If we could speak privately, please? We won't take long."

The other woman glanced at Lottie. Clearly she hoped she wasn't going to be dismissed, but Lottie nodded. "All right. Helen, would you mind?"

Helen obviously minded like crazy, but she was too polite to say so. "I'll visit with Mabel and Letitia for a bit. Perhaps they heard something scandalous at the fashion show yesterday."

After she'd gone, Amanda took a moment to study Charlotte Donovan. Like just about every other woman in the room, she was wearing a silk jogging suit. Hers was turquoise with a jagged hot pink streak across it. A hot pink visor held back long, silky brown hair. She wasn't wearing earrings or a tennis bracelet, but the diamond engagement ring on her left hand had to be at least three carats, and that was without counting the channels of smaller diamonds set alongside the pear-shaped primary stone. Amanda was surprised she could lift her hand off the table. Somehow, though, she managed to hoist her drink for half a dozen quick sips. Apparently she hoped the straight bourbon would prepare her for the difficult questions to come.

Amanda decided to be blunt. "Mrs. Donovan, do you know where Margaret is?"

Heavily lashed brown eyes blinked rapidly, then remained hooded. The better to lie, no doubt.

"No," she responded sharply. "Why would you ask? What is your interest in all of this anyway? I wasn't aware that *Inside Atlanta* reported on missing persons."

"Only when there's a bigger story around the disappearance," Amanda conceded.

"What story?"

"From what her husband tells me, this is a pattern. He seems to think my readers will find the explanation for that pattern fascinating. I have to admit I can't help wondering why a woman would repeatedly take her child and run away from a husband who can clearly offer her the world."

Lottie showed not the slightest hint of surprise that Amanda had spoken with Hamilton Kenilworth. Maybe well-bred

Southern belles were schooled to refrain from outward displays of shock.

"That's something you'd have to ask Margaret," she said tersely. "Her private decisions are none of my business." She belted down another half-inch of bourbon.

So, Amanda thought, Lottie wasn't quite as calm about all of this as she was trying to let on. In fact, there was an unmistakable edge to her voice. Perhaps all was not as rosy with the Donovan-Kenilworth friendship as Amanda had been led to believe.

"Her mother says you and Margaret are best friends, that she would frequently turn to you when she felt the need to hide away."

"Not this time," Lottie Donovan said curtly. "Now, if you'll excuse me, I really must ask you to go. I'm being rude to my guest." To make sure Amanda and Jenny Lee got the message, she gestured to Helen, who practically raced back, probably on the off chance she could pick up a clue about what had been discussed.

Amanda plunked a business card on the table, then scribbled her home number on the back. "If you do think of something or if you speak with Margaret, would you let me know?"

Lottie didn't indicate by so much as a nod whether she would. The fact that the business card stayed right where it was was probably not a good sign.

Only when she and Jenny Lee were back outside and safely on their way did Amanda dare to voice what she'd been thinking. "Did you get the impression that Lottie wouldn't care if Margaret fell into a pit of vipers and never showed her face in Atlanta again?"

"Not exactly the attitude you'd expect from a best friend, was it?" Jenny Lee said.

"I suppose she could have been trying to protect her from having her life spilled all over the pages of a magazine," Amanda said, trying to live up to her commitment not to jump to any more hasty conclusions.

Jenny Lee scowled at her. "Amanda, I really hate it when you try to go all objective. You know that woman has a vicious streak a mile wide and we just got a glimpse of a teensy part of it. If she'd say things like that to two total strangers, just imagine what she's saying to dear old Helen right about now."

"You're probably right. One thing's clear, though. If I had Hamilton Kenilworth for a husband and Charlotte Donovan for a best friend, I think I might very well skedaddle out of town, too."

"What are we going to do now?"

"I don't know about you, but I have a sudden need to see my husband and remind myself how nice it is to have a warm, supportive man in my corner."

Jenny Lee's eyes widened. "You're going home for a quickie in the middle of the afternoon?"

Amanda grinned at her. "Yes, Jenny Lee. I do believe that is exactly what I'm going to do."

That trip to the country was just about the smartest thing Amanda had done in weeks. The fields were fallow. Donelli was spending his days catching up on paperwork, reading farm journals and making rare use of his private investigator's license by doing an occasional skip-trace investigation. Pete, after a show of great reluctance back in September, was actually in school. Which meant Amanda had no difficulty whatsoever luring her husband into bed and keeping him there for quite some time.

"Not that I'm complaining," he said when they were snuggled together, exhausted, Amanda's head resting on his chest. "But what brought this on?"

"I was reminded earlier today how lucky I am."

Dark brown eyes studied her intently. "What's the story?"

She described her day, from the early morning encounter with Hamilton Kenilworth, right on through the disconcerting conversation with Lottie Donovan. "Maybe I'm not doing anyone any favors by trying to find this woman. What do you think?"

"Why did you decide to do it in the first place?"

"Because of a snapshot. The way Hamilton Kenilworth was looking at his child in that picture really got to me."

"Has that changed?"

"No."

"Then I'd say you have to keep looking."

"There was something else, too. Thinking about how messed up that family is made me think about Pete. Maybe it's time we start checking into his background more thoroughly. I know we've called all the missing kids hotlines and he's not on them, but that doesn't mean someone somewhere isn't desperately looking for him."

Donelli cupped her face in hands that had grown hard and callused from farmwork, but which were still capable of the gentlest touches in the world. "You know how he's going to feel about that. He's refused to tell us one single word about his past. He may run away if we press too hard."

Amanda drew in a deep breath. This was something she and Joe had talked about several times, something she had agonized over. The time had finally come to make a commitment. "Not if we tell him we want to find out so that we can clear the way to adopting him."

Donelli's gaze was steady, his brown eyes unblinking as they examined her. "You're sure?"

"That I'm ready to be mother to a streetwise teenager? No. But it's something Pete deserves and it's something you want. I think maybe the anticipation is scarier for me than the reality will be."

Her husband laughed. "Don't count on that. From what I remember of male adolescence, the worst is probably yet to come."

She frowned at him. "Don't try to scare me off at this late date."

Donelli folded his arms around her. "I love you."

"I love you."

"I know. You just proved it."

"Will you talk to Pete?"

"I think we should talk to him together." He glanced at the clock on the bedside table. "In fact, I'd say we'll have an opportunity to do that in another five minutes."

"I suppose it would be psychologically traumatic for a thirteen-year-old to come home and find his prospective parents in bed in the middle of the afternoon," Amanda said ruefully.

"No doubt."

"You're sure about the five minutes, though? He won't dawdle just a little coming up the lane?"

Donelli laughed. "Pete does everything at ninety miles an hour. He never dawdles."

Amanda sighed. "Yeah, I noticed that." She let her gaze roam over her husband's naked body one last time. "Too bad, though."

"It surely is, Amanda. It surely is."

They made it into the living room with seconds to spare.

Pete came bounding into the kitchen, letting the screen door slam behind him, shouting at the top of his lungs.

"In here," Joe called back.

When the teenager skidded to a halt in the living room, he already had a handful of cookies and a glass of milk with him. He stared at Amanda in amazement. Amazement quickly turned to wariness.

"You okay? You didn't get chased by some bad guy or something?"

"Nope. Just came home early for a change."

"You sick?"

His attitude was testament to Amanda's workaholic tendencies. "Nope, never better," she told him cheerfully.

"I don't get it."

"I just wanted to see my family."

A sudden grin of understanding spread across his face. "Uh-oh, you guys want me to go out and come back in again? Maybe a couple of hours from now?"

Amanda felt a fiery blush creeping into her cheeks. This was what she was letting herself in for, she reminded herself. She was about to commit to raising a kid who was thirteen going on thirty, a kid from whom there would be absolutely no secrets. She must be out of her mind.

"Actually we've been waiting for you," Donelli said. "Sit down for a minute."

The color immediately drained out of Pete's face and was replaced by an expression of panic. "What did I do?"

Sometimes they forgot that Pete's show of self-confidence was all bravado. Inside, he was one terrified kid, always afraid he was just one step away from being sent away. "Nothing," Amanda reassured him at once. "We've just had an idea and we want to discuss it with you."

He finally sat down, but he was on the edge of the chair, as if preparing to take flight at any second. "Okay, what is it?"

"We'd like to look for your family," Donelli said bluntly.

Pete was on his feet in a heartbeat. "No way, man. Forget it. You guys start messing around in my past, I'm out of here."

"Even if we're doing it so we can get permission to adopt you?" Amanda countered quietly.

Pete was so busy making threats to skip out on them that it was several seconds before he finally grasped exactly what Amanda had said. When it sank in, he simply stared at them. Finally, his voice barely above a stunned whisper, he said, "You really want to adopt me? Like forever? I'd be your kid?"

"That's what we're hoping," Donelli confirmed. "How would you feel about that?"

Amanda had never before seen such conflicting emotions on one boy's face. There was a brief flare of hope, a hint of astonishment, followed by an expression of dread and then, finally, despair. "Forget it," he said, his voice thick with emotion. "It'll never happen."

Before they could argue that anything was possible if they all wanted it badly enough, Pete whirled and ran from the house.

Shaken, Amanda stared after him. "What has he been through?" she whispered. "What could have been so terrible that he will give up everything we're offering just to keep us from learning about it?"

"I think it's time we found out," Joe said grimly.

"Even though it's obvious he doesn't want us to know?"

"Yes."

She regarded her husband worriedly. "What if it drives him away?"

"Then we'll just have to find him and bring him back. After all, aren't we both experts at finding people who don't want to be found?" He pressed a kiss to her forehead. "It'll be okay. In the meantime, I think I'd better go and try to have a talk with him."

"Tell him we love him, no matter what."

When Donelli had gone, Amanda sighed heavily. It had been one hell of a day. First little Lauren Kenilworth, now Pete. Two children whose lives had been shaped, for better or worse, by events far beyond their control. For whatever her efforts were worth, she resolved then and there to do what she could to make things right for both of them.

CHAPTER

Five

With Pete sullen and silent, Amanda lingered at home in the morning far longer than usual, hoping he would open up and talk to her. He'd refused all of Donelli's overtures the night before, hadn't come to the table for dinner. This morning he'd refused breakfast. For a boy with Pete's nonstop appetite, that signaled just how low his spirits had sunk. At least he hadn't run away. She supposed that was something for which they could be thankful.

It was almost time for the school bus when he finally made an appearance in the kitchen. Keeping his gaze averted, he headed straight for the door.

Amanda prayed for guidance on the best way to handle this. "Pete?"

His thin shoulders, clad in a favorite T-shirt and a denim jacket, visibly stiffened. Ignoring Amanda, he jerked the door open.

"Pete?" she repeated more insistently.

"I gotta go. I'm late. I've got a test first period today."

She doubted that taking a test mattered all that much to a boy who hadn't even wanted to go to school a few weeks ago. She went along with the excuse, though. "Okay. Can we talk later?"

He stilled for just an instant, looking indecisive and miserable.

"Please."

"Maybe. I guess," he conceded eventually and with obvious reluctance. "Look, I'm outta here. I'll catch you later." The screen door slammed behind him.

Amanda's heart ached for him. If she had thought it would do any good, she would have kept him home, test or no test, and tried to force him to talk things through, but she knew better. Apparently Pete had learned early that actions spoke louder than words. From the very beginning, when he'd been part of a scheme to deceive Amanda and Donelli, his actions had contradicted his smart mouth. Even as he'd tried to con them, he'd unobtrusively looked out for Amanda.

Since moving in with them, he had been quick to come to Amanda's defense, quick to do Joe's bidding, quick to do anything, except talk about his past. There was no way to tell what scars he bore or whether they were recent or lifelong. There was no mistaking, though, that his trust in Amanda and Joe was a rare gift.

While she was sipping her fourth cup of coffee of the morning and pondering the best way to prove to him that they had no intention of betraying that trust, the phone rang. A hesitant, yet faintly familiar feminine voice spoke her name.

"Yes, this is Amanda Roberts. Who's calling?"

"Helen Prescott."

The name didn't ring any bells. "Have we met?"

"Yesterday, at the country club. I was with Lottie."

An image of the perfectly coiffed blonde formed in her head. "Yes, of course. What can I do for you?"

"I know you left your card there for Lottie, but she didn't want any part of it, so I took it. I was awake all night wondering if I should call."

"Do you know Margaret?"

"Of course. I could have told you that yesterday if you'd asked."

She sounded miffed. Amanda apologized and meant it. She'd been attempting to be discreet, when what she probably should have been doing was pumping everyone in the whole damned country club for information. Of course they all knew Margaret. Country clubs were tight-knit little social communities of people of similar interests and economic means. Or at least they pretended to be.

"How well do you know her?" she asked belatedly.

"We were all in school together, all in the same sorority. I haven't seen so much of her lately, but I do know some things that might help you find her. Could we meet?"

Amanda's adrenaline immediately started pumping furiously. "Of course. Where?"

"Could you come by the house? I'd rather no one know about this."

"Tell me where it is and I'll be there within the hour." Amanda figured that allowed just enough time to check her makeup and floor the accelerator all the way into Atlanta.

As it turned out, she made it to the Buckhead area in just under fifty-five minutes, a new record. Too bad there was no one to whom she could brag about it. Donelli had fits about her driving, which he deemed reckless. So did most of the policemen she'd met. Some of them had been incensed enough to confirm their opinion by issuing a ticket. Fortunately, none of them had been on the road this morning.

When Helen Prescott answered her door, Amanda was tempted to ask her which makeup she used. There was no indication whatsoever that the woman greeting her in wool slacks, an oxford cloth shirt, and blazer hadn't slept a wink the night before. Her complexion looked flawless, even her eyes seemed bright. Amanda decided maybe contact lenses deserved the credit for the latter. No one was born with eyes quite that shade of shimmering turquoise.

Helen led her into a living room about half the size of the other rooms she'd been in in this neighborhood. But though the house was smaller than those of her friends, Helen's exquisite, understated taste somehow made the effect more impressive. She had turned these rooms into a home, while the others had created showplaces.

A bone china tea service had been set up at a table for two in one of the room's large bay windows overlooking a formal rose garden that must have been spectacular in summer. Even now the scent of roses seemed to fill the air. Amanda wondered how Helen Prescott had pulled that off, then noticed the dried rose petals in a crystal bowl sitting on a nearby table.

"Tea?" Helen asked.

Amanda figured she was going to be floating in the stuff by the time she stopped interviewing the women in this crowd. Worse, she was beginning to be able to tell the difference between Earl Gray and English Breakfast tea.

"Why not?" she said, seating herself across from Helen. When she'd accepted the cup of tea, she took one polite sip, then put it aside. Earl Gray. "Now, then, you said you had some information that might help me to locate Margaret. How did you know she was missing, by the way?"

One delicate brow arched to create an expression of disbelief. "Please, Ms. Roberts. Do you suppose there is anyone in this crowd who can sneeze without the rest of us finding out about it?"

Amanda grinned. "In other words, even the best-kept secrets aren't really secret. They're just not spoken above a whisper."

"Something like that."

"So everyone is aware that Margaret has taken off?"

"Undoubtedly. Not that anyone gets too overwrought about it. She does this all the time."

"But her husband says she's been gone longer this time, that she hasn't made contact with any of the people she might usually speak with."

Helen shrugged. "I couldn't say. She wouldn't call me, anyway. We haven't been on the best of terms since . . ." She seemed to reconsider whatever she'd been about to say. "Well, in some time now."

"Since when?" Amanda prodded.

"It was silly, really, just a misunderstanding."

"About?"

"It happened about seven or eight years ago, before she married Hamilton. I warned her not to go through with the wedding."

"Why?" Amanda's gaze narrowed. "You weren't in love with him yourself, were you?"

Helen's laugh was mirthless. "Oh, dear heavens, no! But I have known the Kenilworths all of my life. Hamilton and I were at each other's birthday parties as toddlers. We went to all of the same debutante balls, though he was never my escort. At any rate, I heard things, saw things that confirmed my own judgment. I told Margaret all of that. She resented my interference. Like you, she assumed I must be one of Hamilton's spurned lovers."

Amanda was having trouble following all of these oblique charges. "What exactly did you tell her? And why wouldn't she have known about the same things if you both grew up in the same crowd?"

"Margaret dated someone totally unsuitable in college. She never had a debutante season, absolutely refused a coming out party. During that time there were things she might have heard about Hamilton, but she wouldn't have witnessed any of the incidents."

"What incidents?"

"Hamilton is an extraordinarily possessive man. Obsessive, in fact. His jealous rages were frightening."

Amanda tried to reconcile what Helen Prescott was telling her with her impression of the man who had come to her office the day before. She couldn't.

"You're thinking that you've never met anyone more in control of themselves, aren't you?" Helen guessed. "More careful, more deliberate?"

"Yes."

"That's what made the rages so terrifying. They were so sudden, so explosive, so out of character."

"And yet Margaret married him. Have you ever seen him lose control with her?"

"Amazingly enough, no. Nor have I ever heard even a hint that he might be an abusive husband. Apparently he has faith in Margaret, has faith in their marriage. Up until now, apparently she's given him no cause to be jealous."

"Not even with these little jaunts she takes to be alone?"

"Apparently not. I believe he panicked the first couple of times and called the police, but more recently he's apparently come to accept that this is just something Margaret has to do. She was always a little odd, a little out of step with the rest of us. Hamilton has always seemed quite tolerant of that. If he's in a dither this time, it's because something has drastically changed."

"But you think you might know where she is?"

Helen nodded. "There's a place she goes whenever she wants to be alone. She's been going there for several years now. It's at the beach."

Disappointment rose in Amanda. "In Hilton Head? Apparently everyone has already looked for her there."

Helen laughed. "Oh, my, no. Of course she wouldn't go anyplace so obvious. I'm sure Hamilton and her daddy were swarming all over Hilton Head within hours after she'd disappeared. No, she bought herself a little cottage a bit farther up the South Carolina coast in a place she was certain no one in our crowd would ever think to look."

"Surely, though, her husband knows about it."

"I don't think so. I'm fairly certain she bought it with money she inherited from her grandmother and that she kept it secret even from Hamilton."

"But she told you?" Amanda was having difficulty believing that this woman—whom no one in Margaret's family had even mentioned—knew things about her that even her closest friends and family hadn't guessed.

"Not exactly," Helen said, looking faintly embarrassed. "It's just that she needed someone at the bank to help her close the deal. My husband took care of it for her. Jerrald let it slip one night, then swore me to secrecy. I never even told Margaret I was aware of it."

"But you do know where the cottage is?"

"I don't know the exact address, but it's at the north end of Myrtle Beach." Helen gave a delicate little shudder. "I can't imagine how she can stand it there with all those crowds in the summertime, but then Margaret almost never runs off to hide there in the summer. This time of year the beach itself must be quite deserted. Of course, the golf courses are a draw all year long, but golf was never Margaret's thing."

Amanda tried to envision the kind of despair that would have sent Margaret Kenilworth into hiding at a cottage she'd kept private from everyone she knew. "Has she ever taken anyone there? Is there anyone else to whom your husband might have mentioned it?"

"No, usually Jerrald is quite protective of client confidentiality. How long would he last in banking, if he weren't? If Margaret asked him to keep this transaction just between the two of them, he would have done so."

Amanda decided not to point out that if he'd let it slip with his wife, he might have let it slip with someone else. "But maybe someone else in your crowd works at the bank, maybe saw a record of the deal." She considered the crowd with which she was dealing and amended her guess. "Perhaps someone on the board?"

"I doubt it. From what I understand, it was a matter of transferring the cash to a bank over there. There might have been a record of the transfer, but not what it was for. A board member would have no reason to see such records anyway."

"What about Lottie Donovan? Does she know about the cottage?"

Helen shook her head. "I think perhaps that next to Hamilton, Lottie is the last person Margaret would have told."

Something in her voice alerted Amanda that there was more

to the claim than what she'd actually said. It confirmed her impression from the day before that those two women were not nearly as buddy-buddy as people had assumed.

"Why is that?" she asked carefully. "Mrs. Clayton assured me that Margaret and Lottie had been friends since childhood."

Helen twisted a hankie into a knot. Finally she drew in a deep breath. "I would never say this if I weren't so terribly worried about her," she said with a defensive note in her voice. "I really do despise gossip."

"Of course."

"It's just that for quite some time now I've been aware of certain things, of certain undercurrents . . ."

At this rate, they were going to grow old before Helen worked up the courage to say whatever was on her mind. Amanda bit her tongue and waited.

"I think it is entirely possible that Margaret was having an affair with Lottie's husband," Helen finally said in a rush, then sat back looking guilty. "Oh, dear, I hope this will stay just between us."

So, patience did have its rewards, Amanda thought triumphantly. She kept her voice perfectly even, as if such revelations were everyday occurrences.

"For now, of course, I will keep this to myself," she reassured her worried source. "And even if it becomes relevant to what's happened and needs to be reported, I won't reveal who told me. I would need confirmation for that anyway. Right now, you're just speculating, isn't that right? Or is it more than just those undercurrents you mentioned that convinced you this is true?"

"I . . . well, I happened to see them together one night at the country club. They were arguing. It was so passionate."

Her gaze met Amanda's. "Do you know what I mean? A squabble between two people who are just friends never stirs such passion. Never."

Amanda got the picture. She wasn't wild about it. "When was that?"

"About a month ago." Helen hesitated, her eyes widening as something apparently occurred to her. "Actually," she said softly, "that was the Saturday right before Margaret disappeared."

CHAPTER
Six

L ess than an hour later, intrigued by the information
    Helen Prescott had bestowed on her, Amanda exited
    the elevator at work. Before she could head to her
desk, she saw Jenny Lee waving frantically off to her left,
out of sight of the main newsroom. She detoured in that
direction.

"What's up?" she asked.

"Kenilworth is in Oscar's office pitching a hissy fit about
this magazine's maverick reporter. That's you, in case you
didn't know."

"Me?" Amanda echoed incredulously. It wasn't that the
label was unfamiliar or even insulting, it was just that this
was one of those rare times when she felt it was totally
undeserved. "He started this investigation himself. He sat
right next to my desk in there and poured out his heart about
his missing daughter and errant wife and pleaded with me to
help him find them."

Jenny Lee shrugged. "Apparently he figured that entitled

him to okay every step of your investigation. He seems to think you're talking to all the wrong people."

"In other words, I haven't gotten back to him for more of his interpretation of events," Amanda guessed.

"Actually I think he's offended that you never got back to him at all, not even to say you'd do the story."

"That's the breaks. How's Oscar taking it?"

"He looks as if he's about to shoot somebody." Jenny Lee paused thoughtfully. "I think, though, that he'd prefer to aim for Kenilworth's stuffed shirt."

Amanda grinned. "In that case, maybe I'll join the fun."

She found Hamilton Kenilworth, wearing yet another perfectly tailored suit, silk blend shirt, and impressive cuff links, pacing Oscar's office in yet another pair of spotless loafers. Brown leather this time, to go with the tan and cream tones of the rest of the ensemble. Amanda couldn't be sure if he was pacing because he was irritated or because there was still no place to sit.

Oscar was observing this release of pent-up energy with his usual disgruntled expression. He seemed relieved when he spotted Amanda in the doorway.

"There you are," he said heartily. "Mr. Kenilworth was just expressing his displeasure over the way in which you are researching your latest story."

Amanda turned a cool gaze on the man in question. His eyes were blazing, a sure sign that something she'd done in the past twenty-four hours had genuinely ticked him off. "What's the problem? I thought you were desperate to get my help in locating your wife. I thought you'd be pleased that I took the initiative and got right on it."

"By talking to her parents? The Claytons hate my guts."

"I spoke with Mrs. Clayton," Amanda corrected. "I don't

believe she mentioned any real animosity toward you. She is terribly worried about her daughter, though."

"What about Lottie Donovan? Why did you have to drag her into it?"

Amanda determinedly clung to a reasonable tone. "You told me that your wife hadn't been in touch with her best friend. I wanted to confirm that."

"My word wasn't good enough?"

"Frankly, no." Before he could launch into another tirade, she decided she'd better explain a few facts about the way she worked. "Look, Mr. Kenilworth, perhaps we'd better get something straight here. You came to me with an idea for a story. I finally came around to your way of thinking. Now the ball is in my court. I talk to anyone with information. I go wherever the story takes me. You don't get to manipulate the outcome. That's the way journalism works."

He regarded her with obvious indignation, then whirled on Oscar. "There! Do you see what I mean? She's out of control."

"She's doing what we pay her to do," Oscar corrected. "She's an investigative reporter for this magazine, Mr. Kenilworth. Last time I looked, your name wasn't on the paychecks around here."

"I brought this story to her—"

"Your motivation continues to puzzle me, though," Oscar said, regarding him thoughtfully. "You out to destroy your marriage or what?"

"I'm looking for my daughter," he retorted. Again there was an almost indiscernible pause before he added, "And my wife."

"How's she going to feel about seeing your personal problems splashed all over a magazine? Trotting out all your dirty laundry for your friends to see doesn't seem like the best way to get a reconciliation. I know what my wife would do. She'd take me out and hog-tie me, then shoot me with the first weapon she could get her hands on."

Kenilworth looked appalled by the very idea. "Violence is not Margaret's way," he insisted stiffly. "I suppose you could say she makes use of passive resistance. She just vanishes."

"You hoping to embarrass her into coming home?" Oscar asked. "Most women really hate being publicly humiliated. Most men, too, for that matter." He studied Kenilworth speculatively. "That doesn't bother you? How's it gonna look when people find out that such a high-falutin' attorney can't keep his own house in order?"

"It's a price I'm willing to pay to get my daughter back. As for Margaret, as I told Ms. Roberts, Margaret should have thought of the consequences before she left home."

Amanda had an idea, but she was hesitant to use her trump card this early in the game. Still, she needed to know exactly how much Hamilton Kenilworth really knew about what was going on with his wife . . . and how angry he might be about it.

"Is Gilbert Donovan in town?" she asked, drawing stares from both men in the room. Oscar looked puzzled. Unfortunately, so did Kenilworth.

"Why would you be asking about Gil?" Kenilworth inquired.

She shrugged. "Just wondering."

"What did Lottie say to you about her husband?"

Amanda didn't even have to feign innocence on that one. "Absolutely nothing," she said honestly. Helen was the one who'd filled her head with that particular tidbit of gossip.

"Then I'm afraid I don't understand why you'd bring up

his name. He has nothing to do with this. You really are way off base here, Ms. Roberts."

Amanda just shrugged. "I figured since Lottie and Margaret are so close and you and Gil are partners, then the four of you must be pretty tight."

"Not especially. I've always found Lottie to be particularly irritating. I can't imagine how Gil or Margaret can stand her. Other than certain essential business and social functions, we spend very little time with the Donovans."

Disappointed at the lack of a more dramatic reaction, Amanda decided she'd better finesse before she was the one responsible for planting any wild ideas in Kenilworth's head about his wife and Gil Donovan. She didn't want to set off one of those jealous rages Helen had alluded to.

"What about the other partners in your firm? Anyone else particularly close to you and your wife?"

"You mean other than my father, naturally," he said with a rather sardonic expression.

"Naturally."

He shook his head. "No, and I really can't see that this is getting us anywhere. I think perhaps coming here in the first place was a very bad idea. Forget all about this, Ms. Roberts. Perhaps I'll leave this in the hands of my private investigator, after all."

She smiled at him. "Sorry. Too late. I find I'm rather fascinated. I'll keep you posted if I discover where your wife and daughter are hiding out," she promised, and made a quick exit before he could get his gaping mouth closed.

There was another explosion of high-decibel arguing, but judging from the way Kenilworth slammed Oscar's door on his departure, Oscar had backed her up. She'd have to remember to thank him.

Unfortunately, her opportunity to do that was right around the corner. She looked up to find her boss glaring down at her.

"What the hell have you stumbled into this time, Amanda?"

"I don't stumble, Oscar. I do very careful research."

"Usually smack in the middle of some hornet's nest," he retorted. "And what the hell was that business about Donovan?"

"I have a source who says that Kenilworth is one very possessive, very jealous man. That same source also said she believes Margaret is having an affair with Donovan. I just wanted to float a trial balloon and see what happened."

"Nothing happened."

Amanda sighed. "I know. Kinda makes me wonder if Kenilworth is one very cool customer or if my source was wrong on all counts."

"What's your gut telling you?"

"I wish I could say that he's some sort of borderline psychotic who goes apeshit with jealousy, but it doesn't track for me. I don't like him. I think he's cold. But I keep going back to that picture of him with his daughter. Nobody could fake the kind of love and tenderness on his face in that picture."

For once Oscar seemed as fascinated as Amanda with the psychological underpinnings of a story. She figured he didn't know what to make of Hamilton Kenilworth, either. The man defied black and white categories.

"Let's not forget that some of the worst killers in history probably had mothers or kids or pets they loved," he reminded her. "Did you notice that he never gets that kind of an expression when he talks about his wife?"

Amanda had noticed. It was the most troubling aspect of the whole thing. Margaret always seemed to be an afterthought, as if he had to make a conscious effort to remember that any search for Lauren must include her. What the devil was going on with that marriage?

"So what are you going to do next?" Oscar asked.

"I have a lead on where Margaret might be. I'm going to follow up on that. I know it's the end of the fiscal year. Do we have any travel money left in case I need to get over to South Carolina?"

"As long as you drive and don't go booking yourself into some fancy tennis resort for a week, we can probably manage it."

"I'm sure I can find some sleazy motel that will suit your idea of thrift without being roach-infested."

He scowled at her. "Have I mentioned that you're awful sassy for a reporter who's barely one week from deadline and doesn't even have a solid lead on a story for the next issue?" he asked pointedly as he walked away.

"My lead is solid," she hollered after him, then added to herself, "Sort of."

She promptly got on the phone to Myrtle Beach information. It was probably too much to hope that Margaret Kenilworth would have a listed phone number. She didn't. But, to Amanda's astonishment, M. Clayton did.

She spent a full sixty seconds debating what she was going to do if Margaret actually answered the phone herself. She didn't really want to get into any of this long distance. Maybe she could just confirm that there was someone in the house, hang up, and hit the road. If she drove like a bat out of hell, she ought to be able to reach Myrtle Beach by nightfall. She hoped a telephone hang-up wouldn't spook Margaret Kenilworth into leaving.

Now, that was a plan, she decided. A solid plan. The plan

of a woman who was finally developing patience. She dialed the number and let the phone ring five times, six, eight, ten. Another incredible display of patience, she congratulated herself.

She was just about to hang up when a child's breathless voice said, "Hello, is anybody there?"

Amanda heard a distant shout in the background. Then before she could react, even to hang up, she heard a woman say impatiently, "Dammit, Lauren, I told you you were never to answer the phone here."

With that the receiver quietly clicked in Amanda's ear, disconnecting her from the missing Lauren Kenilworth ... and her mother.

CHAPTER

Seven

Amanda's first instinct after hearing Margaret and Lauren Kenilworth's voices was to take off for Myrtle Beach the second she'd hung up the phone. Instead, in another display of remarkable patience, she slowed down just long enough to do the responsible thing by calling Donelli to tell him where she was going and to give Jenny Lee an assignment. She wanted her assistant to track down an address to match that phone number for M. Clayton and to do background research on a few more of the players in the whole Kenilworth scenario.

After getting Donelli's blessing and Jenny Lee's promise to have the information by the end of the day, Amanda practically ran to the parking garage. Fortunately, she had a lot of experience with following up on the unexpected. She always kept a packed overnight bag in the trunk for sudden out-of-town assignments.

She was just unlocking the car door when someone emerged from the shadows. With her heart pumping like crazy, she froze, bracing to defend herself. The fight-or-flight surge of adrenaline kicked in with a vengeance.

"Hey, Amanda."

Relief flooded through her as she recognized Pete's forlorn voice, then saw his face. Her heart rate took another thirty seconds to slow to something approaching a normal rate.

"Dammit, Pete, you scared the daylights out of me."

He shuffled his sneaker-clad feet and kept his eyes downcast. "Sorry."

With some effort, Amanda managed to keep her voice stern. "Why aren't you in school? And why the devil were you waiting down here in the garage instead of coming to see me upstairs?"

"I didn't want to bother you. I figured I'd just hang out until you got off."

"That could have been hours from now."

He shrugged. "I didn't have nothing else to do anyway."

Amanda sighed and just barely restrained the urge to reach out and give him a fierce, reassuring hug. She cursed the people who had taught him to withdraw from physical demonstrativeness, the same people no doubt who'd convinced him he was a bother.

"Pete, you're not a bother. Not ever. Don't you understand that yet? Now tell me why you're here."

"I was thinking maybe it was time to move on. I was going to take off, but I didn't want you to worry too much, so I came to say good-bye."

His words killed any chance of a quick getaway. Struggling to find the right tactic to keep him from fleeing, she leaned against the fender of the car and scowled at him. A tough love approach, which allowed for her current mixed emotions of irritation and unconditional acceptance, won out. "Do you honestly think that a quick good-bye will keep me from worrying about you? And what about Joe? Did you say good-bye to him?"

"I figured you could do that."

She shook her head. "No way. You think you're grown-up enough to take off on your own, then you're grown-up enough to tell Joe what you're doing."

"I can't," he said, looking miserable.

"Because you're afraid he'll try to talk you out of it? Sounds to me like you know what you're doing is wrong."

"Nah, that's not it. It's just, you know, he's gonna be real disappointed in me."

"Yes, he will be," she said, refusing to sugarcoat the truth. "He loves you."

Pete stared at her, clearly startled by the blunt assessment of how much Joe cared for him. His expression told her that no one had ever said that to him before, and that came very close to breaking her heart.

"So do I," she added, just to reinforce the message. "Like it or not, Pete, you've become part of our family. I thought that was what you wanted."

"I did. I do. It's just that I never expected you to want to make it legal." He sighed heavily. "No, that's not true. I did. I guess I just didn't realize that would mean me having to tell you about my parents and stuff."

"We've already taken a huge risk by not contacting your family and letting you stay with us this long. It could get Joe and me in trouble, if your family wanted to take us to court," she reminded him.

He gave short of disdain. "Yeah, right, like they're beating down any doors looking for me." He looked at Amanda, his eyes filled with hurt and confusion. "Well, I guess I'd better be going."

Since her words clearly hadn't made the difference she'd hoped for, Amanda made a quick decision. "Any idea where you're going?"

"Not really. I figured I'd just hang out for a while. I know the streets pretty good. I can pick up some odd jobs. I won't starve or nothing."

Keeping her tone a casual match for his, she said, "Well, if you don't have anything in particular in mind, you could come with me."

"Where are you going?" he asked suspiciously. "I'm not going back to the farm. I just told you that."

"I know what you told me. I've got to make a quick trip to Myrtle Beach for a story. It'll probably take a day or two. You could help me out."

Pete fancied himself a budding private eye. He also, even more than Joe, felt someone needed to look out for Amanda. His eyes brightened at once. Clearly the offer had his attention.

"Really? You'd let me help?"

"Why not? It's better than hanging out on the streets, right?"

"You bet." He hurriedly jumped into the passenger seat as if he feared she might change her mind.

Amanda got behind the wheel. "There's just one condition."

He regarded her warily. "What's that?"

She gestured toward the car phone. "You'll call Joe and tell him you're with me."

"Can I tell him it's like a job, sort of?"

She laughed. "Yeah, you can tell him it's sort of like a job.

Just don't expect to get paid. My expense account doesn't include funds for hiring outside help. You get room and board."

"What's board?"

"Food."

He grinned. "All right! I'm starving."

Considering his failure to eat the night before or at breakfast, Amanda wasn't surprised. "We'll make a pass through a McDonald's drive-in as soon as you've finished that call to Donelli."

Fortunately, Joe kept his opinion of this latest turn of events to himself. Amanda overheard no explosion of indignation on the other end of the line as Pete told him he was going along to help Amanda out. She was sure he wouldn't be nearly as reticent once he got her on the line later. If she had to hazard a guess, he'd take a stance suggesting her actions fell somewhere between contributing to the delinquency of a minor and irresponsible parenting.

Pete looked relieved when he was finally able to hang up. "What did he say?"

"He said I'd better take good care of you or he'd have my hide." He regarded her worriedly. "You aren't gonna do anything dumb, are you?"

"I never do anything dumb," she retorted indignantly. "It's just that some things don't turn out exactly the way I envisioned them."

"Yeah, right," Pete said in a tone filled with Donelli-like skepticism.

Amanda precluded any further analysis of her impetuous behavior by turning into the McDonald's lot. A few minutes later, with a bag filled with cheeseburgers, fries, and soft drinks on the seat between them, she headed for the interstate. The food kept Pete silent, allowing her time to plan her strategy for getting Margaret Kenilworth to talk to her. She hoped by the time she arrived in Myrtle Beach, Jenny Lee would have found someone who could tie an address to the phone number Amanda had gotten from information. Directions would help, too. After that, she'd have to rely on her own ingenuity to convince the woman to open up to her.

Amanda glanced over and saw that Pete was sound asleep. For the first time in the past twenty-four hours, he looked at peace.

"What happened to you, Pete?" she murmured aloud, brushing an untamed lock of hair back from his forehead. "And why can't you talk to us about it?"

He stirred restlessly, as if her softly spoken questions had penetrated his subconscious. Maybe, when the time was right, she could use the Kenilworths' troubled marriage to show Pete that a lot of people lived in dysfunctional families and that the kids weren't to blame for their parents' problems.

Dusk was falling by the time she reached Myrtle Beach's main drag, a road which had more T-shirt shops per square foot than anyplace she'd ever been in her life. After pulling into a parking lot, Amanda picked up the phone and called Jenny Lee.

"Any luck getting that address?"

"It didn't take luck, Amanda, just perseverance."

Amanda held back a chuckle at Jenny Lee's indignation. "Is that a yes?"

Jenny Lee reeled it off, along with very precise directions to the beachfront cottage on the northern fringe of the city.

"How about your other research? Anything I need to know before I go chasing after Margaret?"

"I got backgrounds on everybody you asked me to. I think most of it can wait till you get back, except for one thing."

"What's that?"

"Back in college, Margaret got herself mixed up with some guy who wasn't much better than a drifter. He did odd jobs around the campus. Supposedly he was a lot older, but I found out he was just twenty-two. Apparently their relationship caused quite a stir among her friends and at home. Her parents were ready to yank her out of college and send her off to Europe for a year if she didn't break if off."

Amanda recalled Helen Prescott alluding to that time in Margaret's life, though her description hadn't been as detailed. "Did you find out anything about the guy?"

"Just that not long before the end of the school year, he got himself arrested and sent off to prison. He claimed the whole thing was a frame-up, but the prosecutor had an airtight case."

"What was the charge?"

"There were a string of them, starting with hit and run and ending up with manslaughter. They threw the book at him."

An interesting twist, Amanda thought, but she wasn't sure that it had any relevance to what was going on now. "Okay, Jenny Lee. Thanks. I'll check in with you tomorrow."

"Hey, wait a minute. There's more."

"Oh?"

"Tommy Ray Baldwin—that's the guy—got out of jail about six months ago. He's living in Myrtle Beach. Care to guess the address he gave his parole officer?"

"You've got to be kidding me," Amanda muttered.

"This is no joke. He's right in that same house with Margaret. Amanda, you watch your step over there, you hear?"

"I hear, Jenny Lee. I most definitely hear." She hung up the car phone and reconsidered her options. Maybe nighttime wasn't the smartest time to pay an unexpected visit to old

Margaret, who might be sitting at home with a guy who'd just gotten out of prison and probably had a huge chip on his shoulder if he was framed.

"You okay?" Pete asked, eyeing her sleepily.

"Just dandy," she said.

"Amanda, why are we here?"

"You mean sitting in this parking lot?"

"I mean in Myrtle Beach. You never did say."

"I'm here to see if the wife of a very prominent, upstanding attorney in Atlanta is having a secret assignation with an ex-con."

His eyes widened. "I don't think I like the sound of that and I don't even know what an assig . . . assin . . . whatever you said . . . I don't even know what that is."

She grinned at him. "It's trouble, Pete. It is very big trouble."

Pete groaned and slumped down in his seat. "I knew it. I just knew it. Amanda, maybe we'd better call Joe and have him come meet us."

She shook her head. "No time. It's just you and me, kid."

"Amanda . . ."

She held out her hand. "Partners?"

Pete heaved a sigh and took her hand with obvious reluctance. "Partners."

CHAPTER

Eight

*I*t was astonishing how much food a boy of thirteen could pack away. If girls consumed a quarter of that amount, they'd blow up like those Macy's Thanksgiving Day parade balloons, Amanda thought as she toyed with her second slice of pizza. Pete ate five slices as if the three cheeseburgers and fries he'd had at lunch were little more than a very distant memory.

Pete glanced from the last slice of pizza in the pan to Amanda and back.

"Go ahead," she said. "Take it."

"You sure? You only ate one slice, two if you count that one you're poking holes in with your fork."

Amanda put her fork aside. "Take it. There's no point in wasting it. I'm not that hungry."

Pete grabbed the remaining slice, took a bite, then turned to study her, his expression serious. "How come you're not hungry? You didn't eat nothing but a bunch of french fries for lunch. Are you okay? You look kinda funny."

"I'm just thinking about this story. I'm trying to decide whether we should go by the house tonight to make sure Margaret hasn't taken off since I called there earlier."

"Margaret? That's the dame we're looking for?"

Amanda hid a smile. Pete was a huge fan of old Humphrey Bogart and James Cagney movies. "Yes, that's the dame."

He shrugged. "So, let's take a drive by. I can peek in the windows, if you want. You wanna go now?" He gestured with the remainder of his pizza. "I can finish this on the way. I won't choke or nothing."

"I'm sure it won't take you more than another two minutes to finish it right here. I can wait," she reassured him.

Pete affected another Donelli-like expression of skepticism.

"I can," she said, disgruntled that he was questioning her patience. Pete obviously didn't believe her capable of reforming any more than Donelli did. She didn't feel like listing all the examples of her new virtue that she had demonstrated just that day. Waiting for Pete to eat a slice of pizza was a relatively minor test, given the way he naturally gobbled food. He hurriedly swallowed the last bite and stood up.

"Come on, Amanda. You look like you're about to bust a gusset."

She glared at him, but she had to admit she was relieved to be moving again. From the moment she'd heard that Margaret was apparently sharing her house with an ex-lover who also happened to be an ex-con, she had started getting very bad vibes about this whole mess.

Even though it was past the height of the summer tourist season, the main highway through town was jammed with traffic. Most of the hotels offered golf packages that drew golfing fanatics to the area's dozens of championship-caliber courses. Country music had also discovered Myrtle Beach and there were more and more showcases for country talent popping up, drawing even more year-round visitors.

Amanda drove through the crush of traffic with the air of a woman trying to find a hole to slip through to win the Indy 500. Pete, she noticed, was clinging to the edge of his seat, but his eyes were glittering with excitement.

"Whoa!" he squealed when she narrowly missed the bumper of a car on her right as she squeezed past. He sounded as if he were on a thrilling ride at Disney World.

She grinned at him. "Pete, you are much more fun than Donelli," she said as she swerved past another slow-moving sightseer. "He would have forced me to pull over and turn over the keys blocks ago."

"Yeah, well, maybe he has the right idea," Pete admitted. "I mean you are one crazy driver, Amanda."

Unfortunately, things got quite a bit duller as they reached the northern fringe of town. Traffic thinned out, the speed limit increased. "Sorry, sport," she told Pete. "I guess dodge-'em is over for the night."

Pete didn't seem nearly as distraught as she'd expected. He released the breath he'd been holding since they rounded a curve at a speed slightly in excess of the legal limit.

Amanda checked Jenny Lee's directions one more time. She told Pete the name of the street they were looking for. "That should take us over to the ocean."

"No kidding?"

She glanced over, startled by the sound of awe in his voice. "You've never seen the ocean?"

"No way."

"Then this will definitely be an adventure." She hesitated, suddenly thoughtful. "In fact, when you sneak past the Clayton home," she said slowly, "that's exactly what we'll tell them if you happen to get caught. We'll say you've never seen the Atlantic before and you just couldn't wait."

Pete regarded her doubtfully. "That's pretty lame, Amanda."

"Don't worry about it. You have a very honest face. They'll never suspect a thing." She had an instant's flare of guilt over teaching Pete wiles that might be better saved for adulthood. She worried more about involving Pete in something potentially dangerous, then consoled herself that there was no reason to expect anything to get violent. Maybe what Pete needed more than anything right now was to feel that he was vital to her life.

Amanda turned south along the road running parallel to the ocean, driving slowly to check the addresses on mailboxes. M. Clayton's house was in the middle of the block, a modest, old-fashioned shingled cottage that in the dark looked to be gray or slate-blue with white shutters. A trellis with climbing roses, most of them faded now, filled the space between two of the front windows. Towering pine trees shaded the front lawn, filtering moonlight into streaks of silver. All of the windows were dark, with the exception of the two on either side of the trellis. The living room, Amanda guessed.

There were two cars parked in the driveway, a fancy Range Rover and a more sedate, two-door economy car. It didn't surprise her that the Range Rover bore Georgia tags. She couldn't read anything else, but that peach on the tag was a dead giveaway.

"Pete, look in the glove compartment. There should be a flashlight and paper in there. Write down those tag numbers for me."

"How come?"

Amanda didn't have any specific reason in mind, but she'd

learned long ago that it was better to have such detailed notes available than to find herself wishing she'd jotted something down. "We may need them later. They might help us identify who was here."

"Why don't I just go look in the windows the way we talked about?" he suggested, but he did as she asked and retrieved the flashlight and notebook.

"In a minute. As soon as you get the tag numbers." She glanced over as he flipped off the flashlight. "Did you get them both down?"

He squinted as he tried to read the tag of the car parked in front, then wrote down one last number. "Got 'em."

Amanda put the car back in gear and drove down the block until she came to a small apartment complex. She pulled into the driveway, found a space, and parked.

"How about a walk on the beach?"

"All right!" Pete enthused.

They found a path between the buildings that provided public access to the beachfront. It was clearly low tide. The stretch of sand was still wet and packed hard. Pete's eyes widened at the sight of it.

"Wow!" seemed to be about the best he could say.

"It is something, isn't it?" Amanda said, watching the waves gently lapping at the shore. "When I was your age, I used to go to the ocean with my parents and sit there for hours staring out at it, trying to imagine where it would take me. It has so many moods, too. Quiet and still, like now. Violent, with waves crashing. Gentle swells that could rock a baby to sleep." She sighed. "I never tired of it."

"Do you ever miss where you grew up?"

There was a subdued tone in his voice that alerted her that Pete was asking more than an idle question.

"Sometimes," she admitted. "I liked Long Island. I had great parents. That doesn't mean I wasn't glad to get off on my own, first in college, then to work in New York City. I think it's important to get away from home, so you can find out who you are, so you can learn to stand on your own two feet."

Keeping her gaze focused out to sea, she added casually, "Do you ever miss where you came from?"

"Just my dog," he said in a flat voice. "Red Dog would have liked this place a lot. He loved to play in the water. Even a mud puddle. He'd get all wet and then shake himself. It was like standing under a sprinkler."

A flicker of a smile touched his lips, then faded so quickly Amanda almost thought she must have imagined it.

"My mom really hated it when he did that. She always swatted him with a broom."

"She probably didn't hurt him, though. The broom probably scared him more than anything."

Pete shook his head. "It hurt," he said in a voice that was now barely above a whisper. "It hurt a lot."

Amanda choked back a sob that rose in her throat. Trying desperately to keep her voice as casual as Pete's, she asked, "Did she ever hit you with the broom?"

When he said nothing, she glanced at him and saw the tears tracking down his cheeks. "Oh, Pete," she whispered, and started to reach for him. He backed away.

"It's okay," he insisted with a deliberately careless shrug. "I got away. I just wish I could have brought Red Dog with me." A deep, shuddering sigh swept through him, then his expression turned more purposeful. "Where's that house? Let's get to work, Amanda."

For one, heartbroken minute Amanda had forgotten about Margaret and Lauren, had forgotten the damned story. Pete's determined words snapped her back to reality. As she scanned the houses for the Clayton cottage, she made a vow. Pete would never go back to that home, not while there was breath left in her body to fight for him.

Pete spotted the house before she did. He also caught sight of the little girl playing in the sand not far from the back porch in an area illuminated by a spotlight over the backdoor. Pete pointed her out to Amanda. "Is that the kid?" he asked in a hushed tone.

"I think so," Amanda said.

"Want me to talk to her? You know, like one kid to another?"

Amanda grinned. "Say hello, but don't do anything that would frighten her. She's probably been taught not to speak to strangers. If she doesn't respond, leave her alone, okay?"

He gave her a disdainful look. "Do I look stupid or what?"

"No, you definitely do not look stupid. I'll be down at the shoreline wading, okay?"

"Got it," he said.

Amanda forced herself not to look back. The less interested she looked in what was happening up at the house, the better. She didn't want Margaret getting nervous and taking off before she could come back to talk to her in the morning.

It seemed like Pete was gone an eternity, especially since she'd discovered that the water was like ice. She'd get pneumonia if he didn't hurry. Even standing barefooted on the sand gave her goosebumps.

When Pete finally did turn up, Lauren Kenilworth trailed along beside him. She was about seven now, her blond hair tousled by the damp breeze, her cheeks rosy. Sand covered the knees of her jeans and streaked across her face.

"Hey, Amanda, this is Lauren," Pete announced as if Amanda didn't know perfectly well who it was.

"How are you, Lauren?"

"'kay," she said, studying Amanda shyly.

"Are you having a good visit to the beach?"

To Amanda's surprise, the little girl shook her head. "Not really."

"Why not?"

"I miss my daddy."

"He didn't come along?"

"No. Mommy says he has to work."

"Still, I'll bet you and your mom have a good time here. There's lot to do."

She shook her head. "She's too busy with company."

So, Amanda thought, that accounted for Tommy Ray Baldwin. He was there. She decided not to pry for more information in case Lauren decided to report their conversation back to her mother. Kids that age didn't have a clue about censoring their conversation. Even well-meant promises of secrecy could not be counted on.

"Well, maybe we can come by again tomorrow and you and Pete can build a sand castle," Amanda suggested, hoping Pete wouldn't look too disdainful at the idea. "I'll bet you're very good at that, and Pete's never built one before. This is the first time he's seen the ocean."

Lauren studied the older boy with an expression of puzzlement. "How come?"

"Never got a chance before now," he said with a shrug. "It's no big deal."

"I could show you about sand castles and stuff," Lauren offered. "If my mom will let me."

"We'll ask," Amanda promised. "You'd better run along now before your mom misses you and gets worried."

Lauren looked reluctant to return to the house. She looked up at Pete. "You promise to come back?"

"Sure," he said. "First thing in the morning, right, Amanda?"

"Absolutely."

Satisfied, Lauren ran back across the beach. She reached the back deck of the house and stayed there until Amanda and Pete waved good-bye and moved on.

"Thanks for going along with that," Amanda said. "It'll make it easier for me to get in to meet Margaret in the morning."

Pete gave her one of his cocky grins. "Hey, you need me. Haven't I been telling you that since the day we met? Just remember, you'll owe me big-time for playing in the sand with some kid."

"I owe you for more than that. And I do need you," she said, regarding him evenly. "And not just to help out with stuff like this. You remember that, okay?"

Pete looked embarrassed by the sentimental words, but there was no mistaking the pleased smile that came and went in a heartbeat.

CHAPTER

Nine

Pete loved room service. He studied the menu as if it were a racetrack tip sheet and ordered with the expansiveness of a generous host. Amanda had already decided she'd have to cover part of the room cost to keep Oscar from having heart failure. He would be highly skeptical that she alone had managed to run up a hundred-dollar room service tab on an overnight stop in Myrtle Beach.

She could just hear him asking in that booming, confrontational tone of his, "What the hell were you doing spending that much time in the room when you were supposed to be working on a story?"

She figured it was a good thing she and Pete were checking out right after the gargantuan breakfast he'd just consumed or the kid would bankrupt the magazine, to say nothing of what he would do to her reputation. Oscar was very protective of her relationship with Donelli. Any hint that she might not have been dining alone and he would be on her case like a nosy mother-in-law.

Pete cast one last, disappointed look at the menu as they left the room. "Are you sure we can't stay one more night? I didn't get to try those foreign waffle things."

"Belgian waffles."

"Yeah. Are they any good?"

"I'll make you some sometime."

"No disrespect, Amanda, but I've had your burned pancakes and broken eggs. You're not exactly a whiz at fixing breakfast."

She feigned a scowl, though she had to admit there was some merit to Pete's assessment of her cooking skills. The kitchen was definitely Donelli's domain. "Okay, traitor, Donelli will make the Belgian waffles. We have to leave here. With any luck we'll talk to Margaret this morning and wrap this whole thing up. We'll be back in Atlanta by nightfall."

He didn't seem especially pleased by the timetable. Once they were in the car, he finally asked, "After we get back to Atlanta, then what? You gonna make me come back out to the farm?"

His attempt at a nonchalant air failed. Amanda heard the conflicting anxiety and wistfulness in his voice. "I'm not going to make you do anything. It has to be your choice, what you want to do. But Donelli and I want very much for you to come home again."

"It's not my home," he shot back.

"It could be."

He shook his head. "No way. It'll never happen."

"Why are you so sure of that? Do you think your parents would fight us? Could they make a case in court to force you to move home again? Just from the little you've said, it sounds to me like you would have reason enough to ask the court to let you live with us."

Pete regarded her doubtfully. "No court's going to listen to a kid."

"That's not always true. Besides, you're not a kid anymore. You're thirteen. That's old enough for a judge to take your feelings into account."

A faint flicker of hope sparked in his eyes. "Do you really think so?"

Now Amanda was the one trying to maintain an air of nonchalance. "We'll never know unless you're willing to let us at least talk to a lawyer and find out what the chances are for an adoption."

"Would I have to tell him why I don't want to go home?"

"Probably."

He shook his head. "Then it won't happen. I ain't never talking about that." He glared at Amanda. "Never, okay?"

His vehemence spoke volumes. Amanda reached over and squeezed his hand. "Just promise me you'll think about it. Joe and I just want you to be safe and happy."

Giving her a wistful look, Pete said, "Things were going okay before all this adoption stuff came up, weren't they?"

"Yes."

"Then why can't we just leave it alone?"

"I told you why. It could present some serious legal problems for Joe and me."

"What kind of legal problems?"

"Worst case? We could be accused of kidnapping."

He looked shocked by that. "That's nuts. You didn't take me away. I'll tell 'em that I left of my own free will. You didn't even meet me till I'd been gone for weeks and weeks."

She leveled a gaze straight at him. "Maybe we didn't actually kidnap you, but we didn't take you back, either. The law might not differentiate between the two."

"That sucks." He slumped down in his seat then and stared out the window.

"Pete?"

"Yeah," he said without looking at her.

"There's nothing you could tell the lawyer or Joe and me that would make us stop loving you," she vowed quietly. "Nothing, okay?"

She thought she heard him sigh, but that was all. Maybe, given enough time, he would begin to believe her promise and find the courage to open up to them.

When Amanda and Pete arrived at the Clayton cottage, only the Range Rover remained in the driveway. Once again, Amanda parked down the street in the apartment complex lot, so they could approach the house from the beach. It wasn't that she didn't intend to be totally honest with Margaret, Amanda told herself nobly. She just figured it would be less likely to trigger Margaret's suspicions if Amanda and Pete just appeared to be a typical mother and son on vacation. At least for the time being. She promised herself she wouldn't wait too long before revealing her ties to *Inside Atlanta*.

She had bought a bathing suit for Pete in the hotel gift shop, along with a bright sweatshirt that made him look like any other teenager on vacation. Though the sun was bright, the breeze along the shore was chilly, perfect weather to justify her own jeans, sweater, and sneakers. She'd learned her lesson about being lured into that water the night before. Despite the brisk temperature, though, there was a steady parade of people walking along the packed sand.

"What's the plan?" Pete asked when he could finally tear his rapt gaze away from the water. The tide was coming in now, creating bigger waves than those he'd seen the night before. "Awesome," he muttered under his breath.

"Exactly," Amanda agreed, wishing they could spend the whole day simply enjoying the beach. It was obvious Pete had been denied such simple pleasures. A day just for him would have been a wonderful gift. Unfortunately, she had a job to do. Depending on how things went, though, maybe they could stay on one more day for sheer pleasure. She'd even pay for the room and not try to sneak it past Oscar on her expense account.

She drew herself back to the present. "Okay, here's what we'll do. You go up to the house and ask if Lauren's there. I'll come along, introduce myself to her mother, and tell her we're going to be on the beach right in front of the house if Lauren would like to come outside with us. Margaret may not be thrilled with that, since she doesn't know either one of us. I'll suggest she come along, too."

"What if she still says no?"

"You're not giving me much credit for my persuasiveness."

"But what if?" he persisted.

"Then I tell her straight out why I'm here and pray she doesn't slam the door in my face."

"Then what?"

She feigned an exaggerated scowl. "You're a regular little pessimist. You know that, don't you?"

"What's a pessimist?"

"Someone always looking for the worst to happen."

"Joe says you gotta plan for things. He says that being a farmer and being a private eye are alike that way."

Amanda laughed. Pete had it nailed. Donelli did tend to be plodding and methodical, while she was impetuous. It was a constant source of friction between them. "Yes, he would say that, wouldn't he? Okay, then, if Margaret *tries* to slam the door in my face, I will jam my foot in the door and talk like crazy until she finally listens."

Pete didn't seem to consider that much of a plan. "Maybe I can faint or something. She'll have to let you in then. Nobody'd let a kid die right on their doorstep, would they?"

Since he seemed rather pleased with that idea, Amanda didn't tell him that there was no way she was letting it come to that. She'd talked her way past a lot of angry, resentful, tight-lipped people in her time, including a New York judge she had been nailing on a corruption charge. She doubted that Margaret Kenilworth would be any tougher than some of them.

They paused on the sand in front of the cottage. "All set?" Amanda asked.

"Yeah, yeah, I know my lines. Let's just do it before I get spooked. One last thing, though. Do you think this dame is going to buy the idea that a big kid like me would want to play with a baby like Lauren? I don't want her thinking I'm weird or nothing."

Amanda grinned at him. "Trust me. I'll cover that."

Unfortunately, she never had the chance to use any of her fast-talking strategies. As they got closer to the house, Amanda saw that the windows were all shut up tight. There were sand toys—a plastic bucket, shovel, and molds for a turtle and an alligator—on a patio table, though, and a doll was propped up in one of the lawn chairs. Encouraged by the conviction that Lauren would never have gone far without her doll, Amanda rapped lightly on the back door, then pounded harder.

"Looks like nobody's home," Pete said after a couple of minutes.

"But her car was out front."

"Maybe they went somewhere in that other car."

"And left the Range Rover here? I doubt it."

"So what do you think?" he asked. "Do you figure she saw us coming and is hiding out inside, peeking through the curtains until we go away?"

Amanda wasn't crazy about the little note of sarcasm in his voice. He was starting to sound entirely too much like Donelli at his worst. "That's certainly one possibility," she admitted. "Let's walk around to the front. Maybe she drove off while we were down the block parking."

But the Range Rover remained exactly where it had been. Amanda's spirits sank. Maybe Margaret and Lauren had gone off somewhere with Tommy Ray Baldwin, after all. She could take a quick peek in the windows just to be sure. She inched her way past the climbing roses. The flowers might be dead, but the thorns were not. She gingerly pushed one heavily laden, still sweet-scented section of vine aside for a better view.

As she'd guessed the night before, the windows were in the living room, a cozy space with a fireplace and well-worn furniture. More toys were strewn about. If Margaret and Lauren had gone out, it looked as if they'd be back eventually. At the moment, however, there were no signs of life.

"Amanda?"

She heard something urgent and frightened in Pete's voice that had her whirling around. "What is it? Where are you?"

"Over here," he said, beckoning to her from in front of the window on the other side of the front door. He was pale as a ghost.

When she got closer, she also saw that he was trembling. "Are you okay?"

"Just look, all right?"

She stood on tiptoe again and craned her neck to peer at the angle Pete was indicating. "I don't see anything."

"On the floor, way over there, sort of by that arch. You can barely see it."

"See what?"

"A lady's shoe."

Amanda shot a confused look at him. "So?"

"You ever seen a shoe lying around at that angle unless somebody's foot was in it?"

Filled with alarm, Amanda took another look. "Oh, my God," she whispered. "Pete, I think you could be right. We have to get inside."

"Shouldn't we call the cops?"

"We will," she assured him. "From inside."

"But how will we get in?"

"Just trust me and don't watch," she advised, already digging in her purse for a picklock that a generous source had once taught her to use, purely as part of her research, of course. "And don't tell Joe."

Pete rolled his eyes. "Yeah, right, like he'd be surprised that you're breaking the law."

"It's an emergency," she snapped back, just as she finally got the lock to release and the front door to swing open.

It was an emergency, all right. The woman she assumed to be Margaret Kenilworth was sprawled across the weathered, wide-planked wood floors with a gaping, blood-soaked wound smack in the middle of her chest.

When Amanda finally looked up from Margaret's body, she caught Pete's horrified reaction. All of the color had drained out of his face, making his eyes seem huge. He was bent over, moaning and holding his stomach as if he might be about to get sick.

"Pete," she said gently. When he never even glanced away from the body, she put an arm around him and repeated his name more sharply. "Pete, come on. Let's go outside. You need to get some fresh air."

She drew him out of the house and encouraged him to take deep breaths. She watched worriedly. "You feeling better now?"

He shuddered. "I never saw a dead person before. Somebody shot her, huh?"

"Looks that way. My hunch is that she was shot sometime last night."

Away from the body, his color and his innate sense of curiosity returned. "How can you tell that?"

"Because the blood's practically dry and because of the way the body looks." She regarded him intently. "Are you okay now? Would you like to go wait in the car?"

"No," he said at once. "I'm staying here."

"Then can you do something for me?"

"I guess so," he said nervously. "What?"

"When we go back inside, I'm going to call the police." She hesitated before asking, "Can you look around and make sure Lauren isn't somewhere in the house?" She was ninety-nine percent certain Lauren was safely away or she'd never have asked it of him.

The color washed out of his face again. "You don't think she's dead, too, do you?"

"No," Amanda said with more confidence than was probably justified. Something told her, though, that the killer—and Hamilton Kenilworth immediately popped to mind—had probably taken the child. "If she's here, she might be so scared that she's hiding, maybe in a closet or under a bed. She could be wrapped up in a blanket so you'd hardly notice her, so you'll have to look really carefully, okay?"

"I guess," he said stoically.

While Pete bravely went off in search of Lauren, Amanda dialed the police and reported the murder. She stretched the truth by saying that she'd discovered the body when she'd arrived for an appointment. Who the hell was going to contradict that? Certainly not Margaret.

The instant she concluded the call to the police, she dialed Kenilworth, Kenilworth, James and Donovan. "Mr. Hamilton Kenilworth, please."

"I'm sorry. He's away from the office."

"Are you expecting him soon?"

"No, he's not due back until tomorrow. May I take a message?"

"That's okay. I'll call back," Amanda said. She was about to hang up when she had another thought. "What about Mr. Donovan? Is he available?"

"I don't believe so, but I can switch you to his secretary," she offered.

"Would you, please? Thanks."

Unfortunately, Mr. Donovan's secretary couldn't produce her boss, either. She sounded miffed when she had to admit she had no idea where he was or when he would return.

"Thanks. I'll try again later this afternoon."

"You might as well wait until tomorrow. I don't think he's gonna show up at all today," the secretary said, still sounding peeved.

"I'll call back tomorrow, then," she agreed, and hung up without giving her name.

"Interesting. Two of the men in Margaret's life can't be accounted for, and that doesn't take into consideration the ex-con who was allegedly living here," Amanda murmured to herself just as Pete came back. "Any sign of Lauren?" she asked him.

He shook his head. "I looked all around her room. The way things are messed up, it looks as if somebody might have dragged her clothes out of the closet and tried to pack some or something."

Amanda nodded. "I thought as much."

"You think she was kidnapped?"

"Maybe," she said, not wanting to mention the possibility that the child's own father had snatched her after killing her mother.

After encouraging Pete to wait outside, a suggestion he stubbornly resisted, she took a minute then to get a closer look at Margaret. She avoided focusing on that hole in her chest as much as she could.

In her mid-thirties, Margaret had an abundance of professionally streaked brown hair cut in a style reminiscent of Farrah Fawcett's famous mane of hair a couple of decades back. Her skin was lightly tanned, her figure a trim—almost gaunt—testament to long walks on the beach and hours of hard-fought tennis matches, to say nothing of all those aerobics classes. Amanda glanced at Margaret's hands then and noticed that the illusion of perfection ended there. Margaret's unpolished nails were bitten down to the quick, an oddly pathetic contrast to the elegant wide gold band with its huge marquis diamond on her ring finger. So, Amanda thought, it was definitely not a robbery. That ring was probably worth more than some people earned in a year. No thief would be able to resist that kind of temptation.

Before she could do any more speculating, the police arrived, swarming across the front lawn like locusts. The officer who pronounced himself in charge looked like he was maybe twenty-two and still not shaving. Blond, blue-eyed, and thin as a rail, he reminded her of a gangly adolescent. Amanda wouldn't have trusted anyone who looked that young and innocent to follow up on traffic violations.

Identifying himself as a homicide detective, with a drawl thick and sweet enough to pour on pancakes, Robert Foster Claypoole drew Amanda into the living room, gestured to a sofa, then told her she could just call him Bobby. She decided not to mention that such informality didn't inspire confidences the way he probably assumed it did. Quite the opposite, in fact. She wasn't inclined to tell Bobby much more than her name.

"Now, Mandy, honey—" he began.

Amanda cut him off before he could dig himself into one very deep grave. "It's Amanda, *honey*."

He seemed startled by the edge in her voice. Pete snickered.

"Sorry," Bobby said without much of an abject note in his voice. "Why don't you just tell me again what you're doing here?"

"I had an appointment to see Mrs. Kenilworth this morning. When I arrived, I saw that her car was outside, but there was no response to my knocks. Pete peeked in the window and caught a glimpse of Mrs. Kenilworth on the floor. Afraid that she might have fallen and hurt herself and was unable to get help, I decided I'd better come inside."

She thought the explanation sounded fairly reasonable. A little too rehearsed, maybe, but Bobby didn't seem skeptical. So far, so good.

"How'd you get in?" Bobby asked. "Was the door unlocked?"

"Not exactly," Amanda admitted.

"So you broke in," he said with an expression that indicated more respect than outrage. "Now, how'd a pretty li'l thing like you do that?"

Amanda resisted pointing out that her looks didn't have a damned thing to do with her skill at breaking into a house. "A credit card," she suggested matter-of-factly, but he was shaking his head before the words were out of her mouth.

"Not with that lock. I checked it myself."

"Oh."

"You carrying any tools you'd like to discuss with me?"

Apparently he was smarter than she'd thought. That was a very bad sign. "That depends," she said cautiously.

"On what?"

"On whether you consider me a suspect."

He seemed to consider her reticence amusing. "Maybe for a B and E, not a murder. Murderers almost never stick around to call the cops after they've committed the crime." He shot her a disarming grin. "I learned that in my criminology classes in college."

"Oh, really?" Amanda said with an air of disinterest. She was unwilling to concede even for an instant that he'd taken her by surprise.

"Just the same, I wouldn't mind taking a little peek in that purse of yours."

Amanda considered balking on principle, but since Bobby didn't look as if he were anxious to arrest her on any charges, even the previously mentioned breaking and entering, she handed over the purse. No doubt he could have mustered up a good case for probable cause anyway. Withholding it would just waste time.

His eyebrows rose at the sight of the picklocks. "I think I'll just hang on to these, if you don't mind."

"Remember that I gave them to you of my own free will."

"I'm not holding them as evidence," he informed her. "I'd like to think of them as leverage. I figure these little tools might get you to tell me the whole story of what brought you here today."

Impressed with his style, if not his intentions, Amanda shrugged. "They might indeed," she conceded.

"Stick around until I have a chance to talk to the evidence techs, okay?"

"I wouldn't dream of budging, Bobby."

The instant he was out of the room, Pete moved to the spot right beside her on the sofa. "Amanda, I really think we'd better call Joe," he whispered urgently. "That guy acts like he's gonna lock you away."

"No," she said confidently. "He's just trying to get all the information he can about the murder. You heard him. He doesn't suspect me. For heaven's sakes, nobody would take a teenager along if they intended to kill somebody."

"I don't know," Pete said warily. "The woman's dead. You're here. Seems pretty convenient to me. No loose ends to tie up."

When Pete put it like that, Amanda could see his reasoning. Maybe it wasn't wise to put too much faith in Bobby Claypoole's ready forgiveness of her sins. He'd fooled her with his intelligence. Maybe he'd wind up fooling her straight into a jail cell. Donelli would be royally ticked about that.

"Maybe you should see if they'll let you make a call from here," she told Pete. "Here's my calling card. Ask Joe to stick close to home today."

"You mean don't tell him what's going on?" Pete asked.

"Well, we might be out of here in no time. There's no point in getting him all stirred up. You know how he worries."

Pete handed back the calling card as if it were on fire. "Maybe you'd better call him yourself. I'm liable to get it wrong."

This statement from a kid who'd played out an entire deceptive scenario without a single telltale blink of an eye the first time they'd met. Amanda glared at him. "Chicken," she accused.

"I promised," he said stubbornly.

"Promised what?"

"That I'd never lie to him again. I can't go back on my word."

Amanda heaved a sigh. "Okay, you're right. I shouldn't be asking you to cover my butt. I'll call."

"When?"

"In a minute."

"Now, Amanda."

"You know something, Pete? You are displaying an awful lot of Donelli's traits. He'd be proud of you."

Pete perked up at that.

"I, on the other hand, find some of those traits damned irritating."

Pete, blast the little traitor, laughed. "I know."

Fortunately for everyone, Donelli didn't answer the phone. Amanda left a message that there might be just the tiniest bit of trouble in Myrtle Beach and she'd call home later to explain. She suggested he relay that news to Oscar as well.

"What news?" Bobby inquired pleasantly when she'd hung up.

Amanda almost dropped the phone on her foot. "Don't sneak up on a person like that."

"I find it's a useful way to get information. Who'd you call?"

She had no problem with answering that honestly. "My husband."

"And who did you want him to tell about this?"

That was a far stickier area. If she mentioned Oscar, she'd have to mention *Inside Atlanta*. If she mentioned the magazine, he'd want to know what she did there. It was only a short hop from that to full disclosure of everything she'd discovered about Margaret Kenilworth and her tawdry family life. She really hated spilling her exclusive story to the cops before it made its way into print.

"Amanda, honey, you might as well tell me," he said, as if he'd been reading her mind. "I've got grounds enough to keep you sitting around the police station here for hours on end. That might be rough on that boy of yours."

She glared at him. "That sounds suspiciously like blackmail."

"Or coercion," he said agreeably. "I prefer to think of it as playing my trump card. Now all that's left is to see if you're in or out of the game."

Amanda had to admit that her admiration of this naive-looking cop had just crept up a notch. He was certainly full of surprises. He and Donelli would probably adore exchanging interrogation techniques. Donelli's was equally irritating.

And equally effective.

"What exactly did you want to know?" Amanda said in a way that she hoped was indicative of a moderate desire to compromise.

"For starters, you referred to the deceased as Margaret Kenilworth. This house is listed as belonging to Margaret Clayton."

"Same woman. She used her maiden name to buy it."

"Why?" he asked, looking baffled.

Amanda shrugged. "I can't be sure because I never got to talk to her, but I gathered from a friend that she wanted it kept secret from her family."

"She and Mr. Kenilworth having problems?"

"It is my understanding that she and her daughter had left Atlanta without telling Mr. Kenilworth their whereabouts," she said carefully.

"That explains the toys. Are you sure the daughter was here, though?"

"She was here last night," Amanda confirmed.

His gaze narrowed. "I thought your appointment was for this morning."

"I happened to take a walk on the beach. We spoke to the little girl."

"Where is she?"

"Good question. Pete looked around while I called you. She's not in the house."

"So we could have a kidnapping to go along with murder. Terrific. York, get in here!"

An officer appeared who looked even younger than Claypoole. Amanda decided they must be recruiting the force straight out of high school.

"York, Ms. Roberts here says there was a child in the house last night. She's missing now. See if you can come up with a picture and get out a missing person's report."

As much as she would have liked to keep her own photo of Lauren hidden away in her purse, Amanda couldn't do something that would impede an investigation into her whereabouts. She retrieved the picture.

"Bobby, this is Lauren and her father. I'd guess it's about a year old."

To his credit, he didn't waste time asking how she'd gotten her hands on it. He just concentrated on getting the search started. When he was satisfied that things were under way, he regarded Amanda intently.

"Now, then, Amanda, honey, why don't you tell me what you were doing with that picture?"

Amanda could see that the last of her thus far exclusive information was about to go public. She couldn't see that she had any real choice, but she genuinely hated giving this guy one shred of additional information.

"Come on, now," he encouraged. "I can see you're holding back. That won't do anybody a bit of good."

"That's what you think," she muttered, thinking of the big, bold, exclusive stripe across the front of the next edition that she was about to sacrifice. She sighed. She might as well talk. The local media was going to be all over this story like ants at a picnic anyway. Atlanta reporters wouldn't be far behind.

"Okay, I'll tell you. Hamilton Kenilworth gave it to me."

"You and him have a little thing going," Bobby suggested. "I notice his wife wasn't in that picture."

Amanda's scowl returned. "Bobby, did anybody ever tell you that you have a dirty little mind?"

"Afraid not. I prefer to think of myself as being good at math. Two and two most always adds up to four."

"Well, get out your calculator this time, *honey*, because you're way off." Her tongue practically tripped over itself as she brought Bobby Claypoole up to date on everything she knew about the life and times of Margaret Kenilworth. She talked so fast, Bobby had to ask her to slow down several times. She didn't. She figured it was time he learned to keep up.

"Before I give you a couple of last little tidbits, I'd like to strike a deal," Amanda said.

"For immunity? I thought you said you weren't involved."

Amanda rolled her eyes. "Oh, Bobby, Bobby, Bobby. You really do have to stop jumping to conclusions," she said, ignoring the fact that that was a little like the pot calling the kettle black. "I just want you to agree to share a little information in return for what I'm about to give you. Do we have a deal?"

"Depends on the information and what you want in return."

She grinned at him. "No, you don't understand. This isn't

something where I talk and then you decide. You decide now or I take my information out of here with me."

She glanced up just then and saw Pete listening to the exchange from the nearby doorway. He cringed visibly. She tried to give him a reassuring smile, but it didn't seem to do the trick. He still looked worried that he might have to call Donelli any minute now to report her arrest.

Bobby seemed amused by Amanda's tactics. "Okay, we have a deal. As long as it doesn't compromise the investigation, I will tell you what we turn up as a result of your information."

"Thank you." She glanced at Pete. "Do you still have that paper from last night in your pocket?"

Pete slowly withdrew the piece of notepaper and handed it to her. She turned it straight over to Bobby. "The Georgia tag is probably Mrs. Kenilworth's. The second tag number belonged to whomever was in this house last night."

"Well, I'll be," he said, and once again hollered for York. "Run these for me," he instructed the younger officer. "Let me know what you get."

When York had gone off to check the tag numbers, Bobby turned back to Amanda. "What else?"

"I made two calls while I was waiting for you. Hamilton Kenilworth has been out of the office all day. So has Gil Donovan. Neither man's secretary seemed to have a clue where they might be."

Bobby nodded thoughtfully. "The motives and opportunities just keep piling up, don't they?"

The observation silenced conversation for a time. It was York's return that brought them both out of their reveries.

"I got 'em, boss."

Amanda was pretty sure she knew what to expect, which was why York's first words left her virtually speechless.

"The one car, the one that's missing, was a rental. The company says it was taken out about a month ago by Margaret Clayton."

While Amanda was still trying to recover from that bit of news, he tossed in the real bombshell.

"The Range Rover out front, that belongs to some woman named Charlotte Donovan."

Amanda stared at Bobby and York in bemusement. What the hell had Lottie Donovan been doing in Myrtle Beach at a house she supposedly hadn't known existed? More important, where was she now?

Or was it just possible that Gil Donovan had borrowed his wife's car and driven it to an out-of-state rendezvous with his lover?

CHAPTER

Eleven

A manda was sorely tempted to hop in her car and head back to Atlanta, where it seemed probable that most of the likely suspects who would be hearing about Margaret's murder any minute now would soon be solidifying alibis. She didn't believe for a single instant that this had been some random act of violence. That ring on Margaret's finger was a dead giveaway. Too bad the killer hadn't been smart enough to take it.

Though she was anxious to get back to the suspects, there was just one last thing she wanted to know for certain before she left.

"Mind if I look around upstairs?" she asked the homicide detective.

"For?" Bobby Claypoole asked.

"Well, Tommy Ray Baldwin was supposed to be living here. Seems to me like it might be important to see if he left any clothes hanging in the closets or if he took off."

Bobby nodded. "Let's go."

Amanda wasn't wild about having company, but she figured fighting it would be a lost cause. Bobby had a persistent streak that wouldn't quit. He also had all sorts of rules about protecting a crime scene on his side.

Upstairs they found there were three bedrooms, including the one that had apparently been Lauren's. As Pete had described, it was a mess, with clothes and toys strewn about haphazardly. The room next door appeared to be a guest room, decorated with simple furniture that had been painted white. There were shades of blue in the curtains and bedspread, accented with yellow. Nothing masculine about that and not a single shirt or tie in the closet, she discovered when she looked.

The master bedroom, however, was another story. The king-size bed was rumpled, either by a single very restless sleeper or by a couple enthusiastically engaged in sex. Judging from the faintly musky smell that lingered in the air, Amanda guessed the latter.

A quick scan of the dresser drawers—approved by a nod from Bobby—confirmed that a man was sharing the room with Margaret. Jockey shorts, T-shirts, jeans, a box of condoms, white athletic socks, and colored work socks were neatly folded in the bottom row of drawers in the double dresser. Loose change filled an ashtray on the nightstand by the bed. In Amanda's experience, men, not women, deposited their coins like that at the end of the day. Women's change tended to clutter up the bottom of their purses.

"Some man has been living here," she said. "No doubt about that." She glanced at Bobby. "Any idea where this Tommy Ray Baldwin is working?"

"I've got York checking with his parole officer now."

"Mind if I go along when you question him?"

"No way," he said adamantly. "It's totally against procedure. If he's guilty and gets himself a smart lawyer, he could scream bloody murder about me violating his civil rights by dragging the media along when I question him."

"You wouldn't even know about him if I hadn't told you."

He scowled at the reminder. "We'd have picked up on it."

"Sooner or later," she agreed. "Just look at all the time and energy I've saved you."

Before he could reply to that, York came bounding up the steps. "Hey, Bobby, I've got a location on Baldwin."

Bobby held up a silencing hand, his gaze still pinned on Amanda. "It'll take me a couple of minutes to wind things up here," he said. "There's not a thing I can do if you happen to overhear something and beat me to a location. Do we understand each other?"

"Perfectly," she agreed.

"You spook this guy, I'll haul you in," he warned.

Amanda held up her hand. "I'll be on my best behavior. Promise." She dutifully started from the room, leaving a perplexed York staring after her.

"Bobby, what the hell—"

Bobby cut him off. "Where's Baldwin?"

He named a T-shirt factory on the outskirts of town. Amanda didn't wait to hear anything else he might have learned about the ex-con. She raced down the stairs, nabbed Pete from a deck chair on the back patio, and took off for her car. The one flaw in this generous lead Bobby had given her was that it didn't allow for the fact that she had to race three blocks up the beach to retrieve her car. She and Pete were both panting when they got there.

"Amanda, are you escaping or something?" Pete inquired warily, his chest heaving as he tried to catch his breath.

She had to give him credit for not voicing his concern back at the house and trying to stop her. He'd loyally stuck right by her side. "No, I'm just trying to beat the cops in following up on a lead."

Pete's gaze narrowed. "How did you hear about this lead?"

She grinned at him. "First rule of journalism. Never reveal a confidential source."

Fifteen minutes later, after another one of her tire-squealing races over the Myrtle Beach streets, Amanda parked as close to the entrance of the Design Mania T-shirt Company as she could get.

"Pete, why don't you take a look around the parking lot. See if you see Margaret's car. I have a feeling Baldwin might have it at work."

"What are you going to be doing?" Pete asked, looking worried.

"I'm going inside to look for Tommy Ray. The police are bound to show up any second, so I won't have much time with him. I'll meet you back here at the car." She handed him a key so he could wait inside. Suddenly it struck her that Pete had already had a hell of a morning. He looked as if he were taking it all in stride, but maybe she was wrong to assume that.

"Are you okay with all this?" she asked, watching him closely.

He gave her the jaunty, disdainful look she'd anticipated. "What's the big deal? It's a job, right?"

Amanda nodded, fighting to keep her expression perfectly serious. This was definitely a boy after her own heart. "That's right. I won't be long."

Design Mania had apparently expended all of its creative energy on its products. The building was a long, low brick box. The front door, which looked like it could be kicked in by a toddler throwing a tantrum, was painted a dull, weathered gray. Beds of dying marigolds on either side of the door provided the only hint of color.

Inside, Amanda found a tiny reception area with a buzzer and one of those slide-up windows most often found in doctors' offices. The pretty brunette girl who responded to Amanda's buzz was wearing braces and a maternity top. She looked to be sixteen and at least eight months pregnant. Amanda felt like weeping for her, especially when she saw that she wasn't wearing a wedding ring.

Amanda introduced herself—name only, with no reference to the magazine—and explained who she was looking for.

"Gee, I haven't seen him this morning. He usually stops by on break or something to kid around. Let me check in back." The window separating her from Amanda slid shut with a snap. Amanda tried to see what was going on by peering through the heavily frosted glass, but it was impossible.

Her scanty lead time on old Bobby was rapidly ticking away. She was just about to press the buzzer and ask for an update, when the door to the back swung open. A man appeared wearing jeans and one of the company's own products, a gray T-shirt with MYRTLE BEACH stretching across his broad chest in bright turquoise letters. Not exactly an inspired design. He had a lot of gray in his thick black hair and tiny lines around his hazel eyes, but the eyes were clear and sparkled with humor.

"Not often I get a beautiful lady to come calling," he drawled in a lazy way that had just a trace of seduction to it. "What can I do for you?"

"Maybe we'd better sit down," Amanda suggested, gesturing to the two orange molded plastic chairs sitting on either side of a low table adorned with a plastic plant that looked as if it hadn't been dusted since the nineteenth century.

"How 'bout we go outside instead, darlin'? I sure could use a cigarette and the boss doesn't allow smoking indoors. Too much flammable paint around."

Amanda ignored the sweet talk, which apparently came as naturally to this man as breathing. "Sure."

Outside, Tommy Ray lit up, then studied Amanda. "You gonna get around to what you want anytime soon? Doesn't take me long to smoke this thing. When it's gone, so's my break."

Amanda couldn't seem to reconcile the witty, soft-spoken Tommy Ray Baldwin with her image of a drifter who'd supposedly committed a terrible hit and run. "It's just that you're not what I expected," she admitted.

"Sorry to disappoint you. You looking for tattoos and chains?"

She laughed. "Not quite."

"Look, darlin', much as I'd like to stick around and get to know you, my break's only ten minutes," he reminded her.

"Of course. Look, I understand you've been living at a house owned by Margaret Clayton."

His gaze narrowed suspiciously. The traces of good-humored flirtation vanished. "What of it?" he asked, suddenly defensive.

"When were you last home?"

"Who are you? If you're from the state, I'm not in violation of my parole."

"I'm not from the state."

"You checking this out for Maggie's old man?"

"No. I'm a reporter from Atlanta. I came over here to talk with Margaret."

"You think I have her inside painting T-shirts with me?"

"No. Please, would you just tell me when you saw her last?"

"I'll ask you again, why?"

"Humor me."

For an instant it looked as though he might refuse. Amanda couldn't say she would have blamed him, given her refusal to explain why she was asking all the questions. Finally, he gave a careless shrug.

"Okay, it was about ten o'clock last night. The boss called about nine and asked me to work a double shift. I'm on till three this afternoon. Now I'll ask you one more time, what the hell is this about?"

Amanda really hated to be the bearer of bad tidings, but she also needed to see firsthand what Tommy Ray's reaction was to the news. "Margaret's dead," she said bluntly. "Someone murdered her, probably overnight. I'm sorry."

His hazel eyes filled with genuine disbelief. "She was just fine when I left. We'd just . . ."

"Made love," Amanda provided.

He shook his head as if to clear it. "Yes. What happened? Who found her?"

"I did. A couple of hours ago. The police are right behind me. They'll want to talk to you. If you were here all night, you don't have anything to worry about."

He gave her a wry look. "Right. I just spent ten years in prison for another crime I didn't commit. Pardon me if I don't have a lot of faith in the judicial system." He walked away from her then and covered his face with his hands. When he finally turned back, his eyes shimmered with unshed tears. "She didn't deserve this, you know. She was living with a cold bastard of a husband. She was getting ready to divorce him, so we could finally have the life we planned years ago.''

"Had she discussed divorce with her husband?"

He shook his head. "But I think he knew. She was taking more and more of these trips over here and staying longer every time. He had to be getting suspicious.''

Suddenly his face drained of color. "Lauren, where is she? Is she okay?"

"Missing."

"Then it had to be Kenilworth," he said angrily. "Goddamn him. He must have taken her." He pulled a key ring out of his pocket and headed toward the parking lot. Amanda raced after him.

"Where are you going?"

"After Kenilworth."

Amanda reached out and put a restraining hand on his arm. "Don't. Running, even for the right reasons, won't help you with the police. It'll just send them off on the wrong trail. Stay and talk to them. Let them confirm your alibi first.''

"Who's going to confirm it? I could easily have slipped out for a few minutes, said I was taking a break to smoke a cigarette. Nobody watches all that closely at night. It wouldn't take long to drive over to the house, strangle her or whatever, and get back here.''

Relief flooded through Amanda. For some inexplicable reason she didn't want this man to be guilty. Maybe she was turning out to be a sucker for a drawl and sweet-talk after all. "She wasn't strangled."

He grinned at her. "Maybe I just said that to throw you off.''

She regarded him impatiently. "Are you trying to get yourself arrested?"

"I'm just trying to demonstrate why it's more than likely I will be, especially if the Claytons have anything to say about it. They were behind that last deal. I'd stake my life on that."

"You think the Claytons set you up?" she asked, though she realized as she said it that she'd felt all along that they'd probably had a hand in the arrest. No doubt it had been a desperate, if misguided attempt to keep their daughter from running off with someone they perceived would ruin her life. Apparently Tommy Ray thought she sounded skeptical, because he was scowling. His stance seemed more combative, too.

"Let me give you a little lesson in life, sweetheart. Just being rich doesn't necessarily make a person honorable. Quite the contrary, in some cases. People who've been scrambling to get to the top like the Claytons often lose their scruples along the way. Baldwin's rule." He shrugged. "You can quote me on that."

Amanda heard the sound of sirens in the distance and guessed Bobby Claypoole and his entourage of law enforcement buddies were just minutes away. She dug in her purse for a business card. "Will you call me if you think of anything that might indicate who did this to Margaret?"

Baldwin looked surprised. "You don't think I killed her?"

"I get paid to be objective."

"Hiding behind the big media shield," he taunted derisively. "I asked what you *thought*, not what you intended to write."

Amanda hesitated, then said, "For what it's worth, no, I don't think you're guilty."

His mouth curved into a faint suggestion of his more devastating smile. "Your instincts any good?"

She grinned. "So I'm told."

"You heading back to Atlanta now?"

"Yes."

"Let me know what you find out. Concentrate on Kenilworth. He's the one with a stake in getting that kid home. And he sure as hell had an ax to grind with Maggie."

"What stake does he have in Lauren?" she asked, just as Bobby sauntered over.

Baldwin suddenly clammed up. His entire expression shut down, as if he were distancing himself from the interrogation that was about to take place. No doubt he'd had a lot of practice doing that during all those years he'd been locked away for a crime he claimed he hadn't committed.

Amanda tried to listen in on the questioning, but Bobby kept his voice pitched low and his back solidly to her. It didn't much matter anyway. Baldwin said nothing at all.

CHAPTER

Twelve

Pete was leaning against the side of the car observing the whole interrogation scene when Amanda walked over and joined him. His relaxed, faintly arrogant stance mimicked Donelli's laid-back posture so closely, it brought the sting of tears to Amanda's eyes.

"Did you find Margaret's car?" she asked, keeping her own gaze locked on the interrogation that was happening maybe a hundred yards away so Pete wouldn't detect her misty eyes.

"Nope. It's not anywhere on the lot." He glanced over at her. "Do we have to go now?" he asked, sounding disappointed by the prospect of leaving just when things were getting interesting.

"Not just yet," she reassured him. "I want to see if they lead Baldwin away in handcuffs."

They didn't, though Bobby Claypoole did go inside with him, probably to check on the previous night's time cards. Amanda stayed right where she was until the policeman came back outside, alone. He spotted Amanda and detoured toward her.

"I thought you'd be halfway back to Atlanta by now."

"Just wanted to see if you had the case all wrapped up."

"Afraid not. Looks to me like Baldwin has a halfway decent alibi. The time card checks out."

Amanda held her tongue. There was no point in mentioning all the margin for error that Baldwin himself had suggested to her, including the lack of supervision at night. Surely Bobby could figure that much out for himself.

As if he'd read her mind, he added slowly, "Of course, we could be back, if some other evidence crops up pointing to Baldwin. Time sheet shows only one other guy on overnight. He might have a different story to tell about whether Baldwin stayed on site the whole time. We'll be talking to him a little later this afternoon."

"You trust Baldwin not to run out on you?"

"I get the feeling he wants to ID the killer just about as bad as we do. He's convinced it's the husband. Makes a pretty good case for it, too. He's pretty broken up about this. I think he'll cooperate. Unless, of course, it so happens that he offed her, after all." He shrugged a shoulder in the direction of the gate to the parking lot. "That's why York will be keeping an eye on our friend for the next few days."

Amanda had to admit Bobby had surprised her again. Judging from the shit-eating grin on his face, he'd enjoyed doing it, too. It was way past time for her to stop equating slow talk with slow wits, a habit she'd gotten into when she'd first been transplanted against her will to the South by a husband who'd then abandoned her for a college sophomore. Donelli had come along when she'd still been seething with resentment. Although he was a native of Brooklyn, he had embraced the South with enthusiasm. Eventually, through his eyes and with a little help from her co-workers, she'd become more open-minded, but she continued to have these little relapses.

"You will be staying in touch, won't you, Amanda, honey?" Bobby asked.

"I surely will," she said agreeably, slipping into a drawl every bit as thick as his. Lordy, she hated it when she did that, but she'd caught herself doing it more and more frequently. One of these days she was going to wake up a bona fide Southerner and it was going to break her Yankee heart.

After she and Pete were on the road, the teenager glanced over at her, a worried expression on his face. "That guy likes you," he observed.

"Who? Bobby? You've got to be kidding. He wouldn't trust me from here to the state line."

"I didn't say he trusted you," Pete explained impatiently. "I said he likes you. I've been around, Amanda. I know how a guy looks at a girl when he wants to . . . you know."

She knew. He'd made an interesting differentiation and a very perceptive one. Amanda stole a quick look at him. "Why does that bother you?"

"What about Joe?"

"What about him? He's my husband. I love him. That's not going to stop other guys from being attracted to me, I hope."

"Jeez, Amanda," he said, sounding wounded.

"That doesn't mean I like them back," she assured him.

"But you were sort of flirting with him. You did with that Baldwin guy, too. I heard you guys talking. He called you *darlin'* and that cop kept calling you *honey*."

Amanda choked back a laugh. "Pete, have you ever heard

the expression that you can catch more flies with honey than you can with vinegar?"

"Yeah, so what?"

"Kidding around with a guy to get answers, maybe even flirting with him a little, it doesn't mean anything. It's just using a little honey to get information I want." She didn't add that it was almost the only technique that worked when butting headlong into a genuine Southern macho mentality. "And guys like Bobby and Tommy Ray call every woman *darlin'* or *honey*. It wasn't personal."

"And that's okay with Joe?" Pete asked.

"If the shoe were on the other foot, he would do the same thing."

"And you wouldn't mind?"

Amanda considered the question more thoughtfully than she might have if Pete hadn't so obviously been dismayed. "I might mind," she admitted eventually. "But I'd never object. As long as he was just talking and just looking for information. Can you understand the difference between that and real flirting?"

"I guess," he said without much conviction. "Just the same, I don't think I'll mention it to Joe. He might not be so open-minded."

Amanda laughed. "Oh, Pete, I do love you."

His head snapped around at that and his eyes widened. "You really mean that, don't you?" he said with an air of wonder. "I mean you said it before, but then you were trying to talk me into something. This sorta just happened."

Startled by his amazed reaction, Amanda asked, "What did you think Joe and I have been trying to tell you with this adoption stuff?"

He shrugged. "I don't know. I guess I just thought you were doing it because you thought you ought to."

Amanda reached for his hand. She uncurled the fingers he had balled into a fist, and squeezed. "I'll say it one more time. We love you. Whatever you decide you want to do, that won't change. We'll always think of you as family. Okay?"

When he stayed silent, she glanced over. He was biting his lower lip and blinking back tears. She didn't press for a response. She just squeezed his hand reassuringly once again and turned her own gaze back to the highway.

Not until they were on the outskirts of Atlanta hours later did she dare to break the silence. "Pete? Have you thought about what I asked you? What do you want to do? Will you come back to the farm with me?"

He drew in a deep breath, then let it out slowly. "Yeah, I guess. I think until we figure out who killed Margaret I ought to stick close by. You know, just in case."

Amanda nodded, accepting the explanation without comment, even though she guessed it was a pride-saving excuse. "Thanks. I can really use your help."

"What are you gonna do next?"

"I think I'll call Jim Harrison at Atlanta PD and see if he's been contacted about the murder."

Jim Harrison was quite possibly the one policeman in the universe she trusted and respected. He seemed to enjoy jerking her chain as much as the next cop, but he had bent a fair share of rules for her as well. If he knew anything about the Kenilworth investigation, he'd either tell her outright or manage to point her in the right direction without admitting anything he shouldn't. He was smart, diligent, and honest.

Even though it was well into the evening, he was right

where she'd expected to find him, at his desk at head-quarters.

"How's my favorite homicide investigator?" she inquired cheerfully.

"Suspicious," he retorted. "The minute you start talking like that, I know you're up to something. What do you want, Amanda?"

"Does the name Kenilworth make your little heart go pitter-pat?"

He sighed heavily. "I knew it. I knew it was just too good to be true."

"What?"

"I thought just this once I was going to get through an entire investigation without having you dogging my every move. Turns out you were just lying in wait, weren't you?"

"Actually I've been at the scene of the crime," she confessed. "I thought maybe we could trade. I'll tell you all about finding Margaret's body. You tell me all about the suspects you've been chatting with over here."

It took him a long time to answer. Finally he said, "You were in Myrtle Beach? Why?"

"I was working a story. I tracked Margaret down, then went over to do an interview. When I showed up, she was dead."

Harrison groaned. "Meet me for coffee. I'll buy."

"In the morning," she said. "I have to get Pete out to the farm tonight. Meantime, why don't you tell me who you've been talking to. How did Kenilworth take the news?"

"As a matter of fact, we can't seem to find him. Amanda, if you know anything about this guy's marriage, I suggest you spill it now. I've already had a call from a private eye who says he was trying to locate Margaret for Kenilworth. He says she took off with the kid a month ago. It strikes me as more than coincidence that hours after this PI tells Kenilworth where the lady is, she winds up dead."

Amanda was startled that Kenilworth's investigator had remained on the case after she and Kenilworth had had their conversation. Unless Kenilworth had told the investigator about their conversation and suggested that he keep an eye on Amanda in case she tracked down the elusive Margaret. Damn the man, that had to be it.

"Did he happen to mention how he'd located Margaret?" she asked.

"That part was pretty vague. Apparently, though, somebody led him straight to her."

When Amanda said nothing, Harrison sucked in a sharp breath. "Oh, shit, don't tell me that somebody was you."

Amanda had difficulty speaking around the large lump of guilt that was lodged in her throat. "It could have been," she admitted wearily.

"Eight A.M.," Harrison said sharply. "Don't be late."

"Where?"

"The coffee shop near your office," he said. "And, Amanda, I think maybe I'll let you buy after all. Maybe it'll relieve some of that burden of guilt you're wallowing in."

"I doubt it," she said. "I think it's going to take more than the price of pancakes, eggs, and grits to make me feel better about this mess."

When she'd clicked off the car phone, she glanced at Pete, surprised that he had nothing to say. Thankfully, he was sound asleep.

She spent another twenty minutes consumed by guilt. Then she got furious. "Damn Hamilton Kenilworth," she muttered.

If that bastard had used her to locate his wife and child just so he could kill Margaret and snatch his daughter, then hanging wouldn't be too good for him. She'd tie the damned rope around his neck herself.

Jim Harrison looked as if he'd slept at the police station in the clothes he was wearing. But then, he usually did. Amanda studied his lined face and soul-weary eyes. She realized that in all the time she'd known him, she'd never learned a thing about his personal life, or if he even had one.

"Harrison, don't you ever take a vacation?" she asked after she'd ordered toast for herself and shuddered as he asked for eggs, ham, biscuits and redeye gravy, and grits. She'd never understand how Southern men survived past thirty when they insisted on starting their days with all that cholesterol.

"Sure," he said. "I take a vacation every year. Two weeks." He didn't look especially happy about it.

"What do you do?"

"Get together with a bunch of other detectives."

She bit back a smile. "I don't suppose you get together to go fishing or something."

He regarded her blankly. "Why would we do that?"

"For fun, relaxation."

"Do you have any idea how boring it is to sit in some boat or stand on a shore and try to get a stupid fish to bite?"

"That's always been my opinion," she agreed as the waitress served their breakfasts. Harrison dug right into the mound of grits with its little pool of butter in the middle. Just watching him cost her her appetite.

She pressed her point about the fishing. "There are people who find being on the water peaceful. Some even say catching a big one is a challenge."

He shuddered. "Not for me. Now tell me about you and Kenilworth."

She described their first meeting in her office. "Not that you could tell it from his tone of voice or his expression, but I was convinced by the time we'd finished talking that he was genuinely distraught because his child was missing."

"But not his wife?" Harrison said, immediately picking up on her phrasing.

Amanda nodded. "I didn't get the feeling he gave a rip about his wife."

The detective paused, his forkful of eggs halfway to his mouth. "That's not the same as saying he hated her guts."

"That's right. I don't think he cared about her much one way or the other. It was Lauren he wanted back." Amanda suddenly recalled something Tommy Ray Baldwin had said. "The guy who'd been living with Margaret said something to me about Kenilworth having a stake in finding Lauren. Any idea what he could have meant by that?"

Harrison shook his head.

"Have you talked to Margaret's parents?"

He laid down his fork and closed his eyes. "God, I hate going to see people right after they've found out that their child has been murdered. I don't care how old the kid was or what kind of family background it is, nothing takes it out of me like asking questions of people who've just had this terrible shock."

"Do you have kids, Harrison?"

"Two. They're grown now. Their mother did a good job of raising them. God knows, I was never around to contribute much. She left me when they were still in grade school. I can't blame her. I take my work home with me. Even when I don't say a word, it's eating at my gut. Nobody should have to put up with that." He shook his head, as if to rid himself of the memories of his long-dead marriage. "You were asking about the Claytons. They're a mess."

"Who are they blaming?"

"They're convinced it was some ex-con. They said they'd heard he was out of prison and it would be just like him to kill Margaret to get even with them for having him locked away years ago."

"They admitted that they'd been involved in Tommy Ray Baldwin going to jail?" Amanda said, startled that the Claytons would openly admit such a thing.

"Not in so many words, but their righteous tone suggested he'd gotten exactly what he deserved ten years ago and that they might have helped the process along just a little bit. I do believe they are willing to help it along again, if need be. When they found out he was living in that house with Margaret and that he wasn't already under arrest for the murder, they went ballistic. Mr. Clayton was on the phone taking a strip out of the hide of the police chief down there before I could get out the front door. I don't envy the cops in Myrtle Beach."

Amanda figured Bobby Claypoole could take care of himself. She was just about to tell Jim Harrison about two other prime suspects in the case—Gil and Lottie Donovan, whose car was still sitting in Margaret's driveway—when the detective's beeper went off. He eyed the last of his meal regretfully and stood up.

"I'll be right back."

While he was at the pay phone in the back of the coffee shop, Amanda crumbled her second piece of cold toast—the first was already shredded—and tried to figure out what the Donovan car had been doing in that driveway. Had Lottie driven down to have it out with Margaret over the affair

Margaret was allegedly having with Gil? Had Gil gone down anticipating a secret rendezvous with his mistress? And what would either of them have thought after discovering Tommy Ray living on the premises? On the face of it, anyway, his presence would certainly diminish the importance of Gil Donovan in Margaret's life.

Amanda drank some more coffee, hoping the caffeine would kick her brain cells into gear. The presence of the Donovan car in Myrtle Beach simply didn't make any sense. Helen Prescott had been absolutely certain that no one else, other than she and her husband, knew about Margaret's secret hideaway. Surely Lottie hadn't trailed Amanda to Myrtle Beach as Kenilworth's detective apparently had. The car had been at the house when Amanda arrived anyway, so that scenario didn't compute. As for Gil, as far as Amanda knew, he didn't even know of her existence, so she couldn't have led him there.

Lost in thought, she barely noticed when Jim Harrison came back to the table and sank onto the seat opposite her in the booth. When she did look up, she was stunned to see that he looked even more exhausted than before. Downright drained, in fact.

"What was it?"

"The station just patched through a call."

"From?"

"Hamilton Kenilworth, Senior. He wanted me to know that he and his wife have Lauren. She's safe."

Amanda stared at him in astonishment. "They took her?"

He shook his head. "His son dropped her off late last night, asked them to take care of her for a while. He never said a word about Margaret being dead. When Kenilworth, Senior, read the paper this morning, he was stunned. He must be one hell of a lawyer," he said with a trace of admiration in his voice. "You know, the kind who understands what the law is meant to be about, who really believes in right and wrong and justice. He never even hesitated. He got on the phone and called the station."

"To tell you he had Lauren," Amanda said.

"And to tell me that he has a terrible, gut-sick feeling that his son murdered Margaret."

Amanda just stared at Harrison. "He turned in his own son? Based on what?"

"Like I said, gut-sick instinct."

"Did he tell you where you could find him?"

"That's the real killer," the detective said, pulling out a couple of bills and tossing them on the table. "He's at the office. The man's wife has been murdered and he's at the goddamned office doing business as usual. I don't care if he offed her or if someone else did. How cold can a man be?"

With his expression filled with loathing as he contemplated a man who remained totally emotionless, Harrison started from the coffee shop. Apparently he realized that Amanda hadn't budged, because he turned back. "You coming or not?"

Surprised by the invitation, Amanda slowly got to her feet. She wished she felt better about being there when Hamilton Kenilworth was hauled into custody. Something told her, though, that this case was far from over. Not that there weren't occasionally quick and tidy solutions to murder, but she knew in her gut that this wasn't going to be one of them.

C H A P T E R

Thirteen

Kenilworth, Kenilworth, James and Donovan occupied a large brick structure that was more reminiscent of an impressive mansion than an office building. Built nearly a century before, according to the cornerstone, it sat high on an acre of land shaded by oak and magnolia trees and splashed with well-tended flower beds. The parking lot was hidden away in the back, between the building and a dogwood-studded ravine that must have been glorious in the spring. Amanda could imagine how reassuring it must be for clients just to walk along the curving sidewalk to the twelve-foot-high entrance. The whole place practically reeked of success—legal and financial.

"Don't get in the way," Jim Harrison was instructing her as he grimly led the way toward the entrance. "You keep your mouth shut."

"Are you taking him into custody?"

"Not yet. If I were, you wouldn't be anywhere near here. I'm just going to ask a few questions. See how things stack up. Then pass that along to the police over in Myrtle Beach. You can sit in, if you play by the rules and if Kenilworth doesn't object. He says no, you're out. Okay?"

Amanda nodded. She figured since he had his daughter back thanks to her, Kenilworth owed her the privilege of sitting in that office while he chatted with the detective. If necessary, she'd remind him of that.

With all the display of traditional Southern ambience outside, Amanda was startled to find the very modern addition of an armed security guard inside the front door. An impressive barrel of a man, he looked them over, nodded politely, then stood aside while they spoke to the receptionist, who was shielded by what more than likely was bullet-proof glass. Another sad sign of the times.

Only after the receptionist had buzzed Kenilworth's office and nodded at the guard were Amanda and Jim Harrison permitted through the heavy double doors into the interior of the building. Amanda had the feeling that even Jim Harrison's badge wouldn't cut much ice here without a warrant or subpoena behind it.

Behind those impressive doors, Southern hospitality resumed. The welcome mat was definitely out. The carpet was a plush teal, the paintings on the walls were signed landscapes framed in ornate gold, and the solid, dark furniture suggested it had been brought over on the Mayflower, not bought from a bargain office supply company. Again, the impression of taste and old money was carefully maintained.

The receptionist led them to an elevator discreetly hidden in an alcove and whisked them to the third floor. This was apparently where the senior partners were ensconced in understated digs meant to inspire confidence and remind the clients that they were paying those exorbitant fees for the best legal tradition in town, not for a pricey art collection.

Hamilton Kenilworth's office faced the back of the property, probably considered less desirable than the front, but Amanda decided she wouldn't mind peering out at that wooded ravine all day long from those huge, deep-set windows. It was the sort of view just meant for deep contemplation.

"He's stepped in with one of the other partners for just a moment," his secretary told them. The little sign on her desk said her name was Elizabeth Wilshire.

Tall, thin, and in her mid-thirties, she was dressed in a stylish suit that hadn't come off any rack Amanda ever shopped. Ms. Wilshire also had the manners and sophisticated looks of a well-turned-out debutante. She probably typed a zillion words a minute, too. She would really class up the lobby at *Inside Atlanta*, but Amanda doubted Oscar would spring for the salary it would take to lure her away.

"I've told Mr. Kenilworth you're here," she assured them, with no hint that she suspected this was anything other than a social call. She probably treated felons and elected officials exactly alike. Grace under pressure, the watchwords of a true Southern belle.

"Would you care for coffee or tea while you're waiting?" she asked.

"Nothing, thanks," Harrison said, as if he feared accepting it would taint his investigation.

Amanda had no such reservations. She was still desperate for sufficient caffeine to survive the day. "Coffee. Black, please."

"Certainly."

The coffee, in a gold-trimmed china cup, arrived along

with Kenilworth. He nodded politely at the detective and gave Amanda an inscrutable look.

"I imagine you're here about Margaret," he said, stealing Harrison's thunder.

"As a matter of fact, I am," the detective said. "Want to tell me the last time you saw her?"

"I believe it was shortly after midnight yesterday, when I arrived to bring my daughter home," he said without the slightest hesitation. "And just to save time, I will tell you that she was alive when I left. Mad as hell, but alive."

The detective didn't dispute the brazen claim, for the moment. "What had her so angry?" he asked, backtracking to the start of the confrontation, rather than focusing on the ending.

"She didn't want me to bring Lauren back home."

Kenilworth straightened the cuffs of his shirt in a gesture that was apparently nervous habit. It was the only sign, though, of his agitation. Other than that, his words, in fact his whole demeanor, were cool as a cucumber. If this was designed to impress Harrison with his innocence, Amanda could tell it wasn't working. The detective was watching him with an increasing air of dislike. He stayed silent, in a technique Amanda knew was designed to see what Kenilworth would finally say to fill the void.

"She threatened to charge me with kidnapping," he blurted eventually. "Which is ridiculous, of course. We're married. Lauren is *our* child. No court has ever said otherwise. I had every right to bring her home where she belongs."

"How'd you locate her? I understand from several sources that she had been missing for a month."

The lawyer's gaze shot to Amanda, then dropped to contemplate the pyramid he'd just formed with his fingers. He spent a good deal of time choosing his words. "I had an investigator on the case at first. When he had no luck, I turned to Ms. Roberts. Amazingly enough, she was able to find Margaret within a day or so."

Amanda bristled at the suggestion that her investigative skills were ever in doubt. At a warning look from Harrison, who obviously guessed she was about to explode, she bit back a snippy remark and settled back to listen.

"Tell me a little more about your conversation with Margaret," Jim Harrison suggested.

His questioning had a lazy style meant to inspire confidences. Amanda could hardly wait to see how it worked on an attorney who'd probably warned dozens of clients not to be fooled by it. She waited . . . and waited. Kenilworth disclosed absolutely nothing.

"You say she was angry," Harrison prodded.

He leaned forward until he was just about in Kenilworth's face. Amanda could see he was about to switch gears.

"How angry?" he asked. "Did she threaten more than filing charges? Did she try to stop you from leaving? Did she pull a gun on you? Did she perhaps infuriate you so badly that you couldn't help yourself? Maybe you had a gun yourself and in a moment of justifiable rage you pulled it and shot her? Was that the way it went down, Hamilton?"

The whole line of questions was delivered with just a hint of understanding that belied the serious direction. Suddenly he was the priest offering Kenilworth forgiveness. Amanda noticed that for all his quiet, nonchalant delivery, Harrison's eyes were alert for even the slightest change in his quarry.

"I don't own a hand gun."

The words were flat, a let-down after the scenario Harrison had described. Kenilworth's demeanor remained as chilly and tart as a tall, frosted glass of lemonade on a summer day. Amanda had to give it to him, he was damned convincing.

Harrison consulted his notes, then looked back at the man who waited so calmly for the next question. "Was your daughter with you while you argued with her mother?"

"No. I had carried her to the car. She was already asleep again in the front seat."

"Why didn't you just take off then, rather than return to the house to carry on this argument?" Harrison asked.

"Because I had thrown some of Lauren's things into a couple of suitcases. I couldn't carry those and her at the same time, so I had to go back for them."

"How did you get to Myrtle Beach?"

"A friend flew me over in his private plane." His expression indicated he had grown bored with the discussion. He jotted something on a piece of paper and held it out. "Call him, if you like. If that's all, I have a client waiting."

"Not quite. Where is your daughter now?"

Amanda tried to hide her surprise at the question. Wasn't Lauren's presence at the senior Kenilworth's house what had gotten them over here in the first place?

Kenilworth seemed amused by the question. "Detective, I'm sure you are fully aware that my daughter is with my parents. I'm equally sure that it was my father who sent you racing over here to question me. He probably took one look at the headlines this morning and decided I was guilty of the murder, or at least that there was enough evidence to make a case against me. Obviously, he didn't care to be accused of obstructing justice by hiding my role in this tragic event. He's hoping to end his days with an appointment to the federal bench. A nasty little scandal like this could screw up his chances. He has to play this by the book."

"Weren't you concerned about compromising him when you took your daughter there last night?"

Kenilworth's lips curved slightly. "I knew he would do the right thing."

"Did you kill your wife?" Harrison asked bluntly.

Kenilworth shrugged. "I've already answered that, but no. I did not kill Margaret. There was no reason to. I got what I went there for, my daughter."

Amanda glanced at Harrison, seeking permission to ask a question. He shrugged, then nodded.

"Mr. Kenilworth, were you and your wife planning to divorce?"

He laughed. It was a dry, brittle sound. "Hardly. That was the last thing Margaret wanted. I was a convenient excuse to avoid making a commitment. She could engage in her amorous follies without fear of having to deal with the consequences."

"But that wasn't true, was it?" Harrison said quietly. "She apparently paid quite dearly."

A little of the color seeped out of Kenilworth's complexion then and his eyes seemed to go empty. "Yes. Yes, I suppose she did," he said in a low voice marked by a faint, but unmistakable tremor. The emotion in his eyes was turbulent, a startling contrast to his outward calm.

Amanda suddenly recalled what he had said in her office about being a man who was unused to baring his soul. It made that tiny hint of emotion in his voice resonate with meaning. She wondered, though, if he would ever permit himself to shed so much as a single tear for a wife whose foibles he had apparently understood all too well and, she realized now, loved just the same. For the first time since she'd met him, Amanda could believe what she'd heard about his obsessive love for his wife. Pride, not a lack of caring, had probably kept those emotions well hidden from the world for quite some time now.

He stood up and walked them to the door, ever the gracious host, even under these strained circumstances. As they were about to leave, he laid his hand on Amanda's arm. "Ms. Roberts, thank you for leading me to my daughter." His stern mouth softened. "I can't begin to tell you what it means to me to have her home again."

"I'm telling you, the guy gives me the creeps," Harrison said when he and Amanda were headed back toward the skyscraper where *Inside Atlanta* was headquartered.

"You don't really think he killed his wife, though, do you?"

Harrison glanced over at her, his expression filled with astonishment. "You don't?" At her shake of the head, he laughed. "Amanda, you've lost your touch. I'm willing to wager we have the man behind bars within twenty-four hours."

"And out on bail right after that."

"Not in this case. He'll be in custody in South Carolina. No ties to that community. And I don't care what his fine, upstanding reputation is in legal circles here, that won't cut shit over there."

Amanda could just imagine Bobby Claypoole latching on to all the circumstantial evidence and having a field day with it. It wasn't far-fetched at all. She reached into her purse and found the picture that Claypoole had returned to her before she'd left Myrtle Beach. "Take a look at this," she suggested. "Maybe it will put things in perspective for you."

She waved the photo in Harrison's face.

"Dammit, Amanda, I'm driving. Wait till we get to the next red light."

Fortunately, it rarely took long. Two blocks later on Peachtree, they were stuck in a line of traffic waiting for the light to change. She handed over the snapshot, then kept a close eye on the detective's expression.

"Well?" she prodded, when he said nothing.

"He does seem more mellow here," he admitted grudgingly.

"Mellow, hell! The man looks positively rapturous. He adores that child."

"Which makes the motive to kill the woman who'd taken her away all the stronger."

"Oh, please. Would he do something that would send him to jail and leave his daughter completely alone in the world?"

That silenced him. Finally he said, "Maybe he's just arrogant enough to figure he wouldn't get caught."

"Maybe," she agreed. "I could buy that, if he'd done a better job of getting rid of the body. Or maybe making it look like a random killing, a burglary. He's smart enough to know how to pull that off. Instead, you're supposing he took Lauren, tucked her in the car, then went back to the house and blasted a hole through the child's mother and left her there for any passerby to discover."

The detective started to interrupt, but Amanda was on a roll.

"Wait a minute. Let me finish. What if Lauren had gotten out of the car? What if she'd seen her father kill her mother? Would he have been thoughtless enough to risk that?"

"Okay, okay, maybe you have a point," he conceded.

"Several points," Amanda said, warming to the theory that

made someone other than Hamilton Kenilworth the villain. She wasn't crazy about the man, either, but she just didn't see him as a murderer in these circumstances.

Harrison made a sharp turn at the next corner and headed away from downtown.

"Where are we going now?"

"We might as well go chat with that little girl and see what she remembers about last night."

Amanda's thoughts flew to the sweet child she'd met on the beach only hours before her mother had been killed. "You can't mean to interrogate a seven-year-old."

"No," he said agreeably. "Actually, since it's unofficial, I thought I'd leave that to you."

Fourteen

The very prestigious, very proper Kenilworths and the very wealthy Claytons were wrangling like a bunch of competitive football players during a big game. Amanda hadn't heard so many insulting taunts since Donelli had dragged her to a Georgia–Georgia Tech game.

None of the combatants, who hadn't even made it beyond the foyer, with the front door standing wide open, seemed to notice the arrival of Amanda and Detective Harrison.

"You have no right!" Mrs. Clayton shrieked, destroying forever her carefully cultivated image as a sweet, demure magnolia blossom. "Lauren is *our* grandchild. You can't keep her from us."

"Her father brought her here, and here is where she'll stay until he tells us otherwise," Mrs. Kenilworth snapped right back, a fierce, warrior-caliber gleam in her eyes.

Hamilton Kenilworth, Senior—at least that's who Amanda guessed he was, since he resembled an older version of his son—tried to bring order. "Ladies! *Ladies!*"

They quieted for an instant, though they continued to glare at each other.

"There, now," he said with satisfaction. "That's better. I'm sure we can work this out." He glanced at his wife and added in an apparent attempt at pacification clearly directed at all parties, "Mr. and Mrs. Clayton are understandably upset. They have just lost their daughter."

"Don't you dare patronize me, you old prig," Clayton snapped. "Get Lauren down here or I'll call the police and file charges against the two of you."

Amanda glanced at Harrison. How handy that the police were already in the vicinity. He looked, however, as if he'd rather be in Antarctica.

"Folks," he said in a quiet, soothing tone. It couldn't cut through the decibel level the two families had once again attained. "Excuse me!"

He'd turned those two little words into a command, not an apology. Four pairs of eyes, filled with shock, turned on the source of that sharply spoken phrase.

"Who the hell are you?" Kenilworth demanded. His gaze drifted over Amanda, then dismissed her and returned to Harrison.

The detective pulled out his badge.

"You again!" Mrs. Clayton exclaimed. She peered more closely at Amanda. "And Ms. Roberts. Well, I'll be. Just in the nick of time, too." She shot an imperious look at Harrison. It was a look that probably could have quelled General Sherman had he had the misfortune to cross paths with her on his way through Atlanta. "Tell these people they have no right to keep us from our granddaughter."

"Maybe we could all go in and sit down and discuss this," Harrison suggested.

Clayton turned his angry gaze on the detective. "What's to discuss? Right's right. That child belongs with us. That's how Margaret would have wanted it."

"That may be," Harrison said reasonably. "But I don't think we're going to settle that standing here."

Mrs. Clayton, apparently convinced that they were on the side of right and that this fine policeman would see to fixing things, heaved a relieved sigh. "He's right, dear. Let's all calm down and talk this out. I'm sure the Kenilworths want to do what's best for Lauren."

"Exactly," Mrs. Kenilworth huffed.

Amanda doubted the two women saw eye-to-eye on what that would be. She waited with great anticipation to see how Harrison would do in his unexpected role as mediator. He shot her a bemused look just then, as if he weren't one bit certain how he'd gotten himself into this predicament.

Amanda found the gazes directed back at him equally fascinating. Clayton regarded him with undisguised distrust and belligerence. Mrs. Clayton was practically beaming. Mrs. Kenilworth seemed smug. And Kenilworth looked bored, as if he alone realized that in the end this was something the courts, not Detective Harrison, would decide.

Harrison cleared his throat. "Now, then, what I'd really like to do is have a word with Lauren myself."

That suggestion drew four horrified reactions.

"Oh, no."

"I really think that would be inappropriate."

"Absolutely not."

"What kind of monster are you?"

This last came from Mrs. Clayton, who only moments earlier had practically declared the very same man a saint.

Any trace of bemusement fled from the detective's expression. Amanda could see he was back in his element.

"I'm afraid you don't understand," he said mildly. "That wasn't a suggestion. I need to speak with her. If you don't allow me to see her, then you'll just have to deal with the South Carolina police. After all, Lauren may have been the last person to see Margaret alive."

Kenilworth's expression turned grim. "You are suggesting that—"

"I'm not suggesting anything," Harrison corrected. "Your son says Margaret was alive when he left. Lauren may be aware of other visitors who were expected late yesterday."

"It was that terrible Tommy Ray Baldwin who killed her," Mrs. Clayton said. "There's not a doubt in my mind about that. He was always a terrible influence on Margaret. He very nearly ruined her life ten years ago. When that didn't work, he came back and killed her. It's plain as day, he's been holding a grudge all this time."

"I spoke with him," Amanda said. "He blamed you for what happened to him, not Margaret."

"Obviously he knew he could get back at us this way, by worming his way into her life, then murdering her. What could possibly hurt us more than losing our precious daughter? He's had years to plot this revenge."

"Margaret apparently saw things differently," Amanda pointed out, not quite willing to go so far as to mention they were living together. Apparently, though, Mrs. Clayton already knew. Her nose was wrinkled.

"Why she would have been in the same house with him is beyond me. He must have been some sort of Lothario."

Weeping now, she pulled an already crumpled hankie from her purse and dabbed ineffectively at the tears.

Clayton regarded his wife helplessly. "Come, now. Please don't get yourself all upset again." He frowned at the Kenilworths. "How can you deprive us of a chance to visit with Lauren, when she's all we have left?"

Mrs. Kenilworth looked ready to relent. She glanced at her husband. "Hamilton?"

"Perhaps we should allow Lauren to come down and visit with her grandparents. The detective could make his inquiries at that time." He glanced at Harrison. "Would that be acceptable? It would be less traumatic for Lauren that way, I'm sure."

"Of course," Harrison agreed. "Just let me remind all of you now not to try to influence the child's answers."

Kenilworth nodded. "Fine, then. I'll send for her."

"And I'll have cook send in some refreshments for all of us," his wife offered. "Perhaps it will make things seem a bit more . . ."

If she had said *festive*, Amanda might have strangled her herself. Instead, she faltered, then said, "A bit more normal."

While the Kenilworths were gone, an uncomfortable silence fell over the room. The Claytons sagged, as if the debate over seeing Lauren had drained the last little bit of life out of them.

A sedate Lauren finally came into the room, hand-in-hand with her tall, handsome grandfather. Her gaze gravitated at once to her maternal grandparents. She broke free, started to run, then skidded to a halt as if she sensed Kenilworth's displeasure. She continued at a restrained pace into Mrs. Clayton's open arms. Thin arms clung to her grandmother's neck. When she finally pulled back, her cheeks were streaked with tears. "Where's Mommy? They won't tell me where Mommy is."

Clayton shot a look of pure outrage at the Kenilworths.

"Oh, sweetheart," Mrs. Clayton murmured, sitting down with the child and rocking her in her arms. "Mommy had to go away. God needed her."

"I need her, too!" Lauren said adamantly. *"Where is she?"* Her voice rose in a wail of protest.

"In heaven," Mrs. Clayton said. "She's gone to heaven, baby."

As tiny as she was, Lauren seemed to have some concept that heaven was a place from which people didn't return. Choked sobs made her words almost incomprehensible.

"She's ... not ... coming ... back?" Each word was punctuated by a huge, gulping sob. Her eyes were huge and shimmered with tears. "Not ever?"

A lump formed in Amanda's throat and threatened to choke her. She noticed that Jim Harrison's eyes had grown moist as well and he no longer looked nearly as anxious to ask his questions. Unfortunately, police work seldom allowed time to indulge in sentiment. Maybe a distraction would even be good for the little girl, Amanda decided.

"Lauren?" he said quietly. "I'm Detective Harrison."

For the first time those huge gray eyes turned away from her grandparents. She stared at the detective, then noticed Amanda. Eyes far too serious for a seven-year-old and still shimmering with tears studied Amanda unflinchingly.

"I know you," she said finally. "You were on the beach. With that boy. You said you'd be back in the morning."

"That's right," Amanda said, ignoring the stunned expressions around her. She kept her attention focused entirely on

Lauren. "When we came back, though, you'd already left with your daddy."

She nodded. "He came while I was sleeping. He said he was bringing me home. I told him I didn't want to leave Mommy, but he said it would be okay, that she'd be here soon, too." She hiccuped. "But . . . but she won't, will she?"

Amanda shook her head. "No, I'm sorry, baby, but she won't. Did you hear your dad talking to her that night?"

Lauren's sad little gaze never wavered from Amanda, as if dealing with a stranger allowed her to distance herself from the emotions so close to the edge with the rest of her family. She nodded solemnly. "They were yelling. And then I didn't hear any more."

Amanda exchanged a glance with Harrison. "Because your mommy stopped yelling?"

She shook her head. "Because I went back to sleep."

"Where was your mom's friend then?"

"You mean Lottie?"

The question drew startled looks from everyone except Amanda and Harrison, who knew about Lottie Donovan's car being in the driveway.

"Lottie was there?" Amanda prodded.

Lauren nodded. "For a little while. Before dinner."

"Was her husband with her?"

A thumb went in her mouth, a sign that the trauma of the past twenty-four hours was causing her to regress to earlier methods of comfort. She shook her head.

"Did Lottie spend the night?"

Lauren shook her head again.

"Do you know why she left her car there?"

"No." The reply was barely above a whisper.

Mrs. Clayton hugged her grandchild even more tightly. "It's okay, sweetheart. Everything is going to be okay."

Amanda had never gotten an answer to her original question about Tommy Ray. They needed to establish whether he'd been in the house during the evening or at work as he'd claimed.

"Lauren, I need to ask one more question," Amanda said. "You told me your mommy was busy with company a lot. Did you mean Tommy Ray?"

"Him and lots of other people."

"Was Tommy Ray home when your daddy came to get you?"

Oblivious to her grandmother's strained expression, the little girl shook her head. "He had to go to work. Somebody called him and he told Mommy that's where he was going."

Amanda wanted to be absolutely certain everyone was clear on the timing. "So he wasn't home when your daddy came?"

"No."

Jim Harrison chimed in then. "How'd you feel about Tommy Ray, Lauren? Did you like him?"

Amanda guessed he bought the idea that kids tended to have terrific instincts when it came to people.

"He was okay," Lauren said. "He and Mommy laughed a lot. And he bought me stuff." She hesitated.

Amanda caught the troubled look in her eyes. "Was there something else, Lauren?"

"I don't think I should say."

"Why not?"

"Mommy told me it was a secret, just between us."

"I'm sure she wouldn't mind if you told your grandparents."

"I don't think so," she insisted.

Mrs. Clayton stroked her cheek. "It's okay, baby. It's important that you tell us anything you remember."

"Okay," Lauren said, but she sounded doubtful. Obviously all of these new rules about secrets not being quite so secret were confusing to her. "Mommy told me she and Tommy Ray were going to get married and that he would be my new daddy."

If a ticking bomb had been discovered in the middle of the room, the atmosphere couldn't have grown any more strained. All four adults stared at each other. Judging from their expressions, they were all regretting that the issue had been forced.

Now that she'd revealed the secret, Lauren was unaware of the reaction it had stirred. She went on with more. "I told her I already had a daddy, but she 'splained that now I would have two daddies and that would make me a very lucky little girl." She turned a puzzled gaze on Amanda. "Will I still have two daddies now?"

"No. But I know Tommy Ray cares about you a lot. I saw him yesterday and you were the very first person he asked about. I'm sure he'll come to see you as soon as he can."

"Over my dead body," Mrs. Clayton muttered, her expression horrified.

"That's enough," her husband hissed. "Now's not the time."

Jim Harrison stood up then, signaling an end to the talk. He bent over and offered a hand to Lauren. He smiled when she politely placed her tiny hand in his. "Thank you very much, young lady. You've been a big help. Your mother would be very proud of you."

He nodded at the others. "We'll see ourselves out."

Mr. Clayton ignored that and followed the detective and

Amanda to the door. "You find out who shot our daughter," he said, "and I'll write a check to cover the cost of adding another hundred police to this city's force." Though his expression was that of a man who'd been utterly defeated, there was a grim determination in his voice.

"There's no need for that," Jim Harrison reassured him. "We'll do our best anyway."

Clayton waved off the claim. "Hell, I know that. It's just that I have to do something. I don't know the first thing about investigating a murder. Writing checks is about all I'm good for."

"We'll talk again," Harrison promised. "I know how I'd feel if this were my daughter. I wouldn't sleep until it's resolved."

What Amanda knew, but the detective never said, was that he wouldn't sleep until he'd found a resolution for this father, too.

CHAPTER

Fifteen

O scar met the elevator as Amanda finally arrived back at the *Inside Atlanta* offices. "How nice you could drop by," he muttered sarcastically. "Don't they have phones where you've been? Is there some reason why I had to read on the front page of yesterday's paper that Margaret Kenilworth was murdered, instead of hearing about it from the reporter who went to South Carolina to interview her?"

There was no good answer to that, so Amanda withheld her usual snappy retorts. "Sorry. You're right."

For a second she thought the shock of her admission was going to fell Oscar right where he was. He recovered nicely, though.

Still scowling, he said, "You got the interview, though, right?"

"Afraid not. She was dead when I got there."

He groaned. "Exactly what do you plan to write to fill that space I'm holding for you in the next issue?"

Amanda patted his hand. "Never fear. The story's getting

better and better. Lots of sex and violence and obsession. You'll love it."

"I should be so lucky," he said with an air of resignation. "You hate that kind of stuff. You'll water it all down until it's some psychological treatise."

She grinned. "But just think of all the good we'll do. We can give people tips on getting out of negative relationships before they turn violent. I'll have Jenny Lee call some experts today. You know what you're always telling me."

He regarded her with suspicion. "What?"

"We don't control the story. The story controls us."

"When did I ever say that?"

"Well, maybe not in those precise words," she admitted. "I think it was more like, 'Leave those goddamned preconceived ideas at the door!'"

He rolled his eyes. "Okay, okay. Just get in here and tell me what you do have."

Joining him in his cluttered office, which had a new layer of junk on top of the last layer she'd seen, Amanda summed up everything that had happened while she was in Myrtle Beach. She concluded with the events since she'd hooked up with Detective Harrison this morning.

"The only real suspect I haven't seen yet is Gil Donovan," she added. "And I need to get back to Lottie and find out what she was doing in Myrtle Beach and why her car is still over there. I think I'll talk to a lot more people about the Kenilworth marriage while I'm at it. Helen Prescott claimed Hamilton was obsessed with his wife. He contradicts that. He says Margaret was the one who didn't want to let go of the marriage. I'm inclined to buy Helen's version. Somebody told me Kenilworth had some sort of stake in keeping his daughter with him, too. I want to find out what that's all about."

"A trust fund?" Oscar suggested. "Is the guy short on cash?"

"With the kind of law practice he has?" Amanda replied doubtfully.

"Times are tough for a lot of law firms these days. Maybe things aren't as rosy over at Kenilworth, Kenilworth, James and Donovan as they once were."

"I'll have Jenny Lee check that out today, too."

"What are you going to do first?"

"I'll try to locate Gil Donovan. I want to find out exactly where he was when the murder was committed. When I found the body, I called his office. His secretary hadn't seen him all morning and wasn't expecting him in." She shrugged. "Of course, you'd think a lawyer who was guilty of murder would have sense enough to create an airtight alibi, wouldn't you?"

An hour later, back at the law offices of Kenilworth, Kenilworth, etc., Amanda managed to talk herself as far as Gil Donovan's outer office. She glanced at the nameplate on the secretary's desk. Vanessa Donovan. Another Donovan?

"Are you and your boss related?" she asked the perky young woman, whose miniskirted suit displayed an indecent amount of thigh for a business office. To be fair, Amanda conceded that maybe she was just irritated because her own thighs wouldn't withstand such a display.

"We're cousins, twice removed or something like that," Vanessa reported cheerfully. "When I told my daddy I wanted to move to Atlanta, he said the only way he'd let me come was if I took a job right here with cousin Gil, so's he and Lottie could watch out for me."

Amanda was delighted by the discovery that Vanessa Donovan obviously loved to chat. Working in a law office had yet to tighten her lips. "Do you live with them as well?" Amanda asked.

"Why, no. That'd be a real inconvenience. Besides, what's the fun of living in a big city if somebody's always telling you what to do?"

Amanda grasped her point. What she couldn't understand was why her parents thought that cousin Gil's supervision in the office was all this girl needed to keep her safe when what she really needed was to tone down her wardrobe. Amanda decided maybe she hadn't had Pete long enough to comprehend all of the finer points of parenting, especially when it came to precocious teenagers or those who'd just passed beyond those adolescent years.

"Is Mr. Donovan around now?"

The twentysomething woman shook her head, setting a cascade of pale blond hair into languid motion.

"Like I asked Marilou . . ." She tilted her head questioningly. At Amanda's blank expression, she added, "The receptionist downstairs. I asked her to tell you that cousin Gil, I mean Mr. Donovan, is out of the office today."

Amanda figured her next question might put her on trickier ground, at least if Vanessa had even a grain of restraint in her chatterbox mentality. "He was gone yesterday, too, wasn't he?"

"He sure was," Vanessa admitted without so much as a hint of ambivalence. "He and Lottie went out of town."

Together? Amanda wanted to say, but discretion forced her to keep her suspicions to herself. "Oh?" she said in a way that she hoped would lead to more confidences.

"They sure needed a break. Gil works so hard, harder than the other partners, that's for sure," she said, then looked horrified that she'd shared such a comment with a perfect stranger.

In Amanda's estimation the reaction was somewhat belated, but she, for one, appreciated the delay in its onset. She pretended that she saw nothing indiscreet about the remark. Obviously Vanessa had been lonely for someone to talk to. Amanda was more than happy to provide an ear and a little guidance about the direction of the conversation. "They went on a vacation, then? Any idea where?"

Unfortunately, Vanessa's belated sense of caution had kicked in. She regarded Amanda wearily. "Where'd you say you were from again?"

"*Inside Atlanta.*"

"That's that magazine, right?"

Obviously Vanessa wasn't a fan, Amanda decided. She probably wasn't even a reader of anything weightier than *Cosmo.* "It's a magazine," Amanda confirmed.

"And why is it you're looking for cousin Gil?"

"I just have a few questions for an article I'm doing. I'm sure he'd want to give me a quote," Amanda said, guessing from the number of times his name had turned up in her Kenilworth research that Gil Donovan was media savvy enough to instruct his secretary to pass along any requests for interviews immediately. "Any idea how I can reach him?"

"Not exactly. I mean, I know where he probably is. He and Lottie always do the same thing," she said, without giving away any specifics. "It's just that he's told me I'm never, ever to try to get in touch with him when he's on vacation. He always calls in." Her expression brightened. "I could tell him when he does that you're anxious to speak with him. That would work, wouldn't it?"

Amanda shrugged. "That depends on how soon he's likely to call in. Are you expecting to hear from him today?"

"Maybe."

That sounded far too tenuous for Amanda. "Vanessa, honey, I know you're just trying to do your job, but I really think your cousin would want you to point me in the right direction. Couldn't you give me a clue and I'll take it from there?"

Vanessa struggled with her conscience for what seemed an eternity. Finally she said, "I suppose a clue wouldn't hurt. They keep a big ol' boat over in Myrtle Beach. Whenever they want to get away, they take it down to the Bahamas or someplace."

Amanda worked very hard to keep a triumphant expression off of her face. Myrtle Beach? My God, they were smack in the thick of the murder scene.

Now that she'd loosened Vanessa's tongue again, she probed for more information. "How long is this trip of theirs supposed to take?"

"That depends. They usually call once they get to the Bahamas. If it's really busy back here or some old trial date has been set, they'll fly back and hire someone to bring the boat home."

"And they haven't called in yet?"

"I haven't heard a word, and with all the trouble with poor Margaret, I just know they're going to want to get right back here." Vanessa sighed. "They both adored her, you know. In fact, everyone around here is just sick about what happened. A lot of the work's going to fall on Lawrence James's shoulders unless cousin Gil gets back soon. Neither one of the Kenilworths are going to be able to keep up with things."

She lowered her voice and confided, "I saw Mr. Kenilworth,

Senior, earlier today and he looked downright gray. I even told his secretary he ought to see a doctor before that weak ol' heart of his gives out. And Mr. Kenilworth, Junior . . ." She shrugged. "Who can tell with him? I never knew a person who kept things bottled up the way he does. Do you know we have a pool every time he goes to court to see who can guess the outcome of the case based on how he looks when he gets back? I've never seen a bit of difference, that's just how cool he is."

"Do people here like him?" Amanda asked, wondering how anyone could warm up to a person with such a private demeanor.

"I guess you'd have to say we all respect him," Vanessa said thoughtfully. "Everybody knows he's just brilliant."

"But you don't like him?" Amanda prodded.

Vanessa seemed troubled by the question. "It's kind of hard to like someone who never lets down his guard, you know what I mean? I hope you won't repeat that, though. I'd hate for cousin Gil to hear I'm gossiping behind the backs of the partners. He just hates anyone with a loose tongue. Says that's the kiss of death in a law office."

"Don't worry about it," Amanda reassured her. "He won't hear it from me." She pulled a business card from her purse. Vanessa had already given her the one lead she'd asked for, but it never hurt to leave the door open for more, especially since it seemed unlikely she'd be able to locate Gil Donovan on the high seas. "You could help me out, though. The minute you hear from your cousin, could you ask him to call me, if I haven't already tracked him down?"

"Sure, I'll tell him, but like I said, I don't know when it'll be. If the weather's great, he may not check in for days yet."

"Once he gets to the Bahamas, does he stay on the boat or check into a hotel?"

"Oh, he always goes to the same resort. He wouldn't want to miss out on his gambling."

"Do you know which resort?"

"Why, sure," she said, and named one on the outskirts of Nassau.

Amanda bit back her impatience. If Vanessa had imparted that one little tidbit at the beginning, she could have saved them both this verbal fencing routine. "Don't you call him there if there's an emergency?"

Vanessa shook her head. "Absolutely not. Cousin Gil says not to disturb him there, ever."

Fortunately, Amanda wasn't hamstrung by such specific instructions. She was already dialing information in the Bahamas the minute she could get her hands on her car phone.

Unfortunately, Gil Donovan hadn't checked in. Yes, he was expected. No, there was no specific arrival date. Certainly they would pass along a message the very moment he arrived. The front desk clerk couldn't have been more accommodating. That didn't make up for the fact that he couldn't produce Gil Donovan. Amanda hung up, frustrated.

She called home. No answer there, either. Apparently Donelli and Pete were off somewhere, she hoped together. Their reunion the night before had been tense. Pete's promise to return to school today had been hard-won. All three of them had gone to bed very much aware that the uneasy truce could be destroyed by one careless word on any of their parts.

As she idled at a red light, she debated whether she should call it quits for the day and go home to see if she could do anything to mediate between Pete and Donelli when Pete got home after school. Maybe they were better off left to their own devices, she decided finally. The decision left her at loose ends.

Before she could get too anxious over her inability to find a solid lead in the murder, her car phone rang. Between the static and the speaker's low-pitched voice, she could barely hear a word.

"Who is this?" she hollered.

"Damn, Amanda, did you have to blast my eardrum out?"

Jim Harrison, she realized with a smile. "Sorry," she said in a more normal tone. "What's up?"

"Bobby Claypoole is in town," he told her in that same nearly impossible-to-hear undertone.

"What?" she shouted again, convinced that it was a bad connection. "I can barely hear you."

"Claypoole. He's here."

Something in the detective's voice suggested that the Myrtle Beach officer was not in Atlanta to attend a Falcons game. "An arrest?" Amanda guessed.

"Yes, ma'am."

"Who?"

"I'm sorry. I really couldn't say," he said in a way that told Amanda he would say if she would toss out a few suggestions. He wasn't about to spell it out for her where he could be overheard.

She counted out the suspects in her head, the Donovans, husband or wife, or Kenilworth himself. Baldwin was apparently off the police list for the moment, she deduced. He was in South Carolina, not Atlanta, at least as far as she knew. They wouldn't have had to come chasing over here after him. Personally she liked Lottie Donovan, even though it seemed likely she'd been bobbing around in the Atlantic in the family yacht at the time of the murder.

"One of the Donovans?" she suggested hopefully.

"Nope."

Which left only one likely candidate. "They arrested Hamilton Kenilworth?" she said incredulously.

"Yes, ma'am."

"Holy shit!"

"My sentiments exactly," he said. "Gotta go."

With a deadline staring her in the face, Amanda knew she should have been thrilled that the case had been wrapped up so quickly. She should have been rejoicing that a man she didn't much like was about to be put on trial for murdering his wife. She could spin out quite a few pages of fascinating copy just with the interviews she'd done so far. Oscar would be relieved that there wouldn't be an empty space in the middle of the magazine.

There was just one problem. As much as she disliked Hamilton Kenilworth and his pompous airs, she didn't believe for one single second that he had committed the crime. He would not have done anything that would have left his beloved daughter's fate in the hands of those two warring factions of grandparents. Anyone who'd ever met the Kenilworths and the Claytons would have known that.

Unfortunately, Bobby Claypoole had breezed into town, armed with circumstantial evidence and with one goal in mind. She just hoped the South Carolina judicial system moved a little less precipitously.

C H A P T E R

Sixteen

Hamilton Kenilworth looked slightly paler than usual, but that could have been due to the crummy lighting, Amanda decided. He certainly did not look like a man who had just undergone hours of tough police questioning or a man who was about to be carted off to jail for murdering his wife. He looked, in fact, just as unflappable as ever. Even his tie and those tidy French cuffs of his remained precisely in place.

Detectives Harrison and Claypoole reacted with astonishment to Amanda's arrival at the police station. Harrison's reaction was obviously feigned, but he did a credible job of it. She was proud of him.

"You're mighty quick," Claypoole said admiringly. "Some little birdie sing to you?"

"Why, Bobby, honey, what would make you think a thing like that? I'm just one hell of a reporter." She patted her midsection. "Great gut instincts. They're very important in my business."

"And in mine," he said. "What are yours telling you right now?"

"That you've got the wrong person."

He grinned. "Just goes to prove that mine are sharper than yours."

She grinned right back at him. "We won't know that for certain until his trial's over, will we? You can charge him, but you just can't get around that American tradition of presumption of innocence. God bless our founding fathers."

Bobby was apparently in no hurry to back down, founding fathers ideals or not, which suited Amanda just fine. She did love a good challenge.

"Won't get to any trial, if he's smart," Bobby said. "He'll plead out, temporary insanity or some shit like that, serve his time, and be home before that little girl of his gets to high school."

"Sounds terrific, unless, of course, he happens to be innocent."

"He's not," he said flatly. "His fingerprints were all over the scene."

"Weren't Baldwin's?"

"Hell, yes, but he had him an alibi."

"What about Lottie Donovan's? Her car was in the driveway. She must have been there."

"We have some others we're still checking out," he conceded. "But Kenilworth came whizzing over on one of them fancy private planes, whisked his daughter out of that house, had one hell of a row with his wife on the front lawn." He glanced at Amanda. "Neighbors heard that."

"Did they also hear a shot?"

Bobby looked uncomfortable. Amanda sensed a victory was within her grasp. "Did they?" she prodded.

"There's some dispute over that."

"Who shut the door when he left, him or her?"

Bobby was looking increasingly disgruntled. "Now, who would pay attention to a thing like that?" he asked.

"Anybody who was hanging out the window trying to listen to the argument might also get an eyeful of the way it ended," she pointed out.

"Well, they didn't," he said just a mite defensively.

"Face it, Bobby, honey," she said, mimicking his drawl. "What you've got is a lot of circumstantial evidence, unless you can come up with the murder weapon or a witness who saw him pull the trigger."

"We have enough," he said huffily. "We've got extradition papers being drawn up right this very minute."

"Where's his lawyer?"

"He waived right to counsel." At Amanda's disbelieving expression, he added, "He's a lawyer himself. He knows what he's doing."

"Or maybe he just thinks this whole thing is so ludicrous that he's not taking it seriously."

Bobby regarded her intently. "When did you become such a big fan of Kenilworth's?"

"I'm not a fan. I just don't think it adds up . The man was desperate to be reunited with his daughter. Would he kill his wife, knowing that he'd wind up in jail and not see the kid for years and years?"

"Maybe the whole thing with the kid was a smokescreen. Maybe what he really wanted was to catch his wife living with this ex-con. Once he had the evidence he wanted, he blew her away."

Amanda had to admit that was a troublesome aspect of the case. She had to concede a point to Claypoole. If Kenilworth was obsessively jealous, then finding her with Baldwin might have sent him over the edge. He might not have been thinking of the impact his actions would have on his daughter at all.

Amanda glanced across the room and studied the suspect again. Other than his pallor, he looked too damned cool to have flown into a murderous, jealous rage over anyone. Maybe if he'd feared for Lauren's safety . . . Amanda allowed the thought to trail off. It was an idea that needed to percolate a bit longer before she tried it out on any of the police officers or in her own conversations with Kenilworth.

Damn, but she would like to get to him alone for five minutes. She was convinced she'd be able to judge his reactions better than Bobby or any of the others. Of all of them in this room, she was the one who'd spent time with Kenilworth before Margaret's death. She considered herself fairly adept at picking up on nuances, on faint changes in behavior that went undetected by others. She'd picked up on none earlier in his office, but Jim Harrison had been there. She'd need privacy for the sort of subtle exchange she had in mind.

"How about letting me talk to him?" she asked Bobby.

He laughed at the request. "You suppose you're going to wring a confession out of him?"

"Actually, I was hoping he'd point the finger at someone else, just so I could show you up," she shot back.

This new challenge was obviously too much for him to resist. In fact, he didn't even try.

"Sure, Amanda, honey," he said with the cocky self-assurance of the truly one-track thinker. "You go sweet-talk that man to your heart's content. I'm just waiting for paperwork, then I'm hauling his butt back to South Carolina."

Amanda didn't waste a second. She made her way across the room, cleared a spot on a corner of a desk beside the suspect, and perched there. Kenilworth barely seemed to notice her.

"Anything I can get you?" she offered.

He shot her an amused look. "I suppose you could bake a cake with a file in it. The way this case is being handled, I'm going to need one."

The dry humor surprised her. "Cakes aren't my specialty, but I might be able to help you break the case open with something I do know."

"Oh?"

"I'm a damned good investigative reporter. Nobody should understand that better than you. I led you straight to your wife."

"True," he conceded.

"I could turn up the killer the same way."

"But why would you want to help me?"

"Same reason you gave me when you came to the office— a nice juicy story that will sell magazines."

"You're wasting your time."

She regarded him intently. "Are you confessing?"

"Of course not," he said impatiently. "But I've been on the wrong side of this kind of justice in court more times than I care to recall. They'll manage to railroad this case through, just to prove that the upper classes don't get special treatment."

"You're giving up?" she said incredulously.

He shrugged. "For now. I'll fight it on appeal."

"That's nuts. Help me to find the real killer before this goes any further." A tiny suspicion nagged at her. "Or do you figure this is your just punishment because you wanted Margaret dead, even if you weren't the one who pulled the trigger?"

His expression of astonishment was tempered with just a hint of guilt. That look told her she'd nailed it. For all of his blasé attitude about Margaret's lovers, he'd been hurt. Deeply hurt. And maybe one time too often. "That's it, isn't it?"

"What makes you say that I wanted Margaret dead?"

"Maybe not dead," she conceded. "Just out of your life. I think you'd gotten fed up with these little vanishing acts of hers, even more fed up with the amorous adventures you mentioned earlier."

"I never said anything like that."

"True. But in every conversation we had, Margaret was always an afterthought. You talked about your daughter being missing, about wanting your daughter back. *Then* you'd say something like 'and my wife, of course.' You sounded pretty ambivalent about that part."

He sighed then. "Very good, Ms. Roberts. I was tired of it all. I tried on several occasions to discuss divorce with Margaret, but she was adamantly opposed."

"On religious grounds?"

"Good heavens, no," he said with a laugh. "I'm sure Margaret had bigger sins to worry about than divorce. No, she wanted the Kenilworth name and status. I'm not so sure she cared for her own sake, but she knew how important it was to her parents."

Amanda shifted gears, hoping to catch him by surprise and draw an uncensored reaction. "I saw Lauren earlier."

His eyes lit up at once. It was an astonishing transformation, without any hint that he feared his daughter could spill the beans on him. "How is she? Have they told her about her mother?"

"Yes. She's very upset."

"She's still with my parents, though, not the Claytons?"

"Yes. They were adamant about keeping her there."

He gave a nod of satisfaction. "Good."

"I don't understand. The Claytons seem like kind, decent people. Do you object to Lauren spending time with them?"

"Time, no. Living with them? Absolutely, I object to that. I don't want Lauren's ideas about life shaped by the people who gave Margaret her distorted view of the world. She grew up believing she had to marry a man like me, whether she loved him or not, as if one more generation of marriage with a real Georgian would finally win the Claytons the acceptance they'd always wanted. I don't want that for Lauren."

Amanda figured she had danced around the real issue long enough now. "Lauren mentioned something when I talked to her. It doesn't exactly jibe with what you've been telling me."

"Oh?"

"She says her mother told her that she was going to marry Tommy Ray Baldwin, that she was going to have a second daddy very soon."

Kenilworth actually laughed, but again there was little mirth in the sound. "Oh, please. Margaret lived in a dream world when it came to that man. She thought of him as the one great love of her life, the one she'd been forced to sacrifice to marry me. She'd romanticized him all the more, because she felt he'd been the victim of a terrible injustice. The truth of the matter was, though, that she and Baldwin would have lasted about two months, tops, once Margaret discovered how difficult it was to get along on the income of a factory worker."

"No alimony from you?"

"Not if she remarried."

"What about her parents?"

"They threatened to disown her the first time she got involved with Baldwin. Their opinion of him hasn't changed.

They would have sided with me in a custody battle for Lauren under those circumstances."

"I heard Margaret had an inheritance from a grandmother or something. Wouldn't that have helped them out financially, made a marriage between her and Baldwin possible?"

"If she had money of her own, it's news to me. Her grand-mother, though, was not a wealthy woman. If Margaret got anything, I'm sure it was all used up when she bought that house in Myrtle Beach."

"Why would she tell Lauren about her wedding plans, then?"

"She was fantasizing, I suppose. Or she was trying to put her adulterous actions into a better light. After all, living in sin isn't quite such a stigma if she intended to marry the man eventually."

The explanation made sense. Amanda was willing to let it go for now. "I just have a couple more questions," she told him.

"Fire away. I'm not going anywhere," he said with another hint of that unexpected wry humor. "Talking to you is more interesting than counting ceiling tiles."

"I'm so glad I'm able to provide some diversion," Amanda said, unable to hide her irritation at his attitude that this entire ritual was one tired joke. It made her less inclined to sugarcoat her next question. "How's your law practice these days?"

"Flourishing," he said at once. "If you have any doubts, I'll authorize our accountant to let you look at the books. Why would you ask something like that?"

"I'll explain in a minute," she said, though she had a hunch he'd figure it out for himself once she'd asked her next question. "Does Lauren have some sort of trust fund that you have access to?"

His pleasant demeanor vanished in a heartbeat. He leaned forward and glared at Amanda with eyes the shade of gunmetal. "How dare you," he said softly.

Amanda didn't flinch. She met his gaze evenly. "Does she?" she repeated. "I'm sure you can see why I need to ask."

It took a minute, but his gaze wavered first. He sighed. "Okay, yes. As much as I resent the hell out of the question, I can see your point. Yes, Lauren does have trust funds, which were established by both sets of grandparents, as well as one I set up myself. She has to be twenty-one before she can get a dime." He leveled a look straight at her. "In the meantime, I have access to none of them, not under any conditions. Neither did Margaret, for that matter."

"Are you the beneficiary if something should happen to her?" she asked bluntly.

She thought for a second that he was going to explode at that, but he visibly controlled his anger.

"No," he said tersely. "Neither Margaret nor I would get a penny if Lauren died before us. The trust funds would either revert to the estates of the grandparents or, in the case of mine, it would go first to any children she might have or to a charity if she had none."

The responses left Amanda confused. If money wasn't the issue, what sort of stake had Baldwin been referring to when he said Kenilworth needed his daughter back at home? She'd have to call him and try to pin him down on that point.

One last question about the trusts did occur to her. "If you have no control over them, who does administer them?"

"Gil Donovan."

"Why him?"

"Because he's a friend, a colleague, and a whiz when it comes to financial matters."

"You trust him completely?"

His gaze narrowed. "You say that as if you know of some reason I shouldn't."

"Not really."

"Ms. Roberts, I don't believe you. What have you heard about Gil?"

Reluctantly, she relented. "Someone mentioned to me that he and your wife might be . . . involved."

He actually chuckled at that. "Gil and Margaret? Obviously you don't know Lottie. She would have killed him."

Struck by a sudden thought, Amanda regarded him evenly. "Maybe she killed Margaret instead."

CHAPTER

Seventeen

Locating the Donovans jumped to the top of Amanda's priority list. Unfortunately, another call to the Bahamas proved fruitless. They still hadn't checked in at the hotel. She wrangled Vanessa Donovan's number from Kenilworth and checked with her to see if cousin Gil had called her. He hadn't.

"Damn," Amanda muttered as she hung up.

"Face it, honey. Your boy's about to take a trip," Bobby Claypoole informed her cheerfully.

"I'm not your honey and he is not my boy," she retorted irritably. "Don't you have anything better to do than aggravate me?"

He settled down in a chair, tilted it onto its back legs, and grinned up at her. "Nope. I ain't had this much fun on a case in years."

"Years?" she said skeptically. "Exactly how long have you been on the force, Bobby?"

"Seven years."

"Which makes you how old?"

"Old enough for you, sweet thing." He winked broadly. "How about you and me grabbing a cup of coffee while I wait for my paperwork?"

Amanda waved her left hand in his face. "The ring, Bobby. I'm married."

He laughed out loud. "Hell, honey, I asked you out for coffee, not sex."

He had a point, she decided, grateful that she'd never been one to blush. Maybe she was overly sensitive because of Pete's complaint that she'd been acting too friendly with men other than her husband, including this specific man. The accusation—made by a thirteen-year-old, for heaven's sakes—was ridiculous. What was the big deal? She'd been trying to pry information out of sources—male sources—for years now. This was no different. Maybe Bobby would drop some hints about why he thought this case was going to be such a breeze to prove in court. Maybe there were facts she didn't know.

"Coffee would be great," she told him. "I'll buy."

He laughed again. "Just to show you what a liberated kind of guy I am, I'll let you. Give me a sec, and I'll be right with you."

He went over to Jim Harrison and said something that had the detective staring at Amanda with a stunned expression. Men, she thought in disgust. Harrison never thought a thing about going out for breakfast or coffee with her, but the second he heard she was going out with Claypoole, he figured hormones had to be involved. She could read it in the speculative look he shot her way.

She marched over to join them. "Give it a rest, Detective. Officer Claypoole has something I want."

The remark, to her chagrin, only added to the air of sleazy speculation, especially when Bobby deliberately winked at his Atlanta counterpart.

"Information," she said, but it was clearly too late to save the moment. "Oh, go to hell, both of you."

She was halfway to the elevator when Bobby caught up with her. He'd jammed his hands in his pockets and was watching her with that look of masculine superiority and amusement that made her want to grind her teeth. Forcing herself to calm down, she drew in a deep breath.

"Mountain out of a molehill, huh?" she said when she could finally speak without screaming.

"Pretty much," he agreed. He slanted a sideways glance at her. "Unless, of course, you are after my body."

"You wish."

He laughed. "How long have you been married?"

"A few months."

"I thought so."

"Meaning?"

"You still haven't worked out all the ground rules. I remember when I first got married I was scared to death to even look at another woman for fear a big ol' bolt of lightning would come straight down and zap me. It took me nigh onto a year before I figured out you can do a whole lot worse before you cross the line. Even then, it's not the lightning that gets you. It's your own conscience." He paused thoughtfully. "Or maybe a rolling pin upside the head."

Amanda glanced at him. "So you're married, too?"

He shook his head and the grin came back. "I'm afraid I crossed the line a bit too often. Flat-out couldn't help myself. Too many women are fools for a man in uniform. My conscience was killing me." He shrugged. "If it hadn't, my wife probably would have before much longer. She 'bout put a dent in that rolling pin. I'm older and wiser now. One of these days I intend to try it again and see if I can get it right."

"Kids?"

"No. That's one of the reasons I want to give it another try. I'd like to have a whole passel of 'em running around underfoot."

"You ever gonna be home long enough to help raise 'em?" she asked pointedly.

"Sure," he said, surprising her. "I might even give up police work and go into practice as a private eye, somewhere where I can work from home and set my own hours. Who knows? Maybe I'll even let my wife work and I'll stay home with the kids." At Amanda's snort of disbelief, he said, "Hey, now, I told you I was a liberated guy."

"Why is it that I have trouble mentioning the words *liberated* and *police officer* in the same breath?"

"Maybe you just haven't met the right police officers."

Amanda thought of the one she had living at home. "That's not exactly true. I'm married to an ex-cop from Brooklyn. Now that you mention it, he struggles with his macho instincts every once in a while, but he's a pretty nineties kind of guy. Maybe he's not one in a million after all. I suppose it's possible there are two of you."

In a nearby coffee shop that catered to police, they found a booth and ordered. While they waited for their sandwiches, Bobby stirred half a dozen packets of sugar into his coffee.

"That must give you quite a buzz," Amanda suggested, watching him.

"I figure I've got a long night ahead," he said. "So,

Amanda, tell me more about your husband and that kid you had with you in Myrtle Beach. Is he yours from another marriage?''

"No. The truth of it is, he adopted us." She explained how Pete had come into their lives. "Now we'd like to make it legal, but Pete refuses to give us any leads on his past. He did admit a few things to me, though, enough to convince me he was probably better off on the streets."

"Abuse?"

"I think so."

"Any idea if he was from around here?"

"Jim Harrison checked the missing persons sheets for him. He never turned up. His name hasn't been on any of the national missing kids hotlines, either. My hunch is his parents didn't much care whether he stayed or went."

"I have some friends who track missing kids for a living. I could see what they suggest about doing a reverse check, if you'd like me to."

"Pete's pretty adamant about us leaving well enough alone."

"You can always tell him I ran the check as part of the murder investigation. Put the blame totally on me."

Amanda considered the offer, but in the end she shook her head. "Thanks anyway, but he'd never buy that. I don't want him to stop trusting us. If he leaves, he won't have anyone in his corner. Adopting him might make things all tidy and legal, but it won't really change the way we feel about him. There's nothing to be gained by forcing it."

Bobby looked worried. "You're absolutely convinced there's no one out there who's desperate to have him home again? Someone who's lying awake nights wondering what happened to his kid?"

"A hundred percent convinced? No. But close enough that I don't need to lie awake nights worrying about that."

Bobby finished his sandwich, gestured to the waitress for more coffee, then leaned back and studied Amanda. A slow, lazy smile crept across his face.

"Go on," he said finally.

"Go on and do what?"

"Ask those questions of yours before you bust a gusset. You've pretty much destroyed that sandwich," he said, glancing pointedly at the crumbled bread and bits of ham and cheese she'd been pushing around on her plate. "Since you didn't come here for the food and, to my deep regret, you're not after my body, that leaves my brain. What do you want to know?"

Since he'd nailed it, Amanda saw no point in mincing words. "I want to know why you're so certain you can get Hamilton Kenilworth convicted of his wife's murder."

"You mean besides motive and opportunity, both of which he had aplenty."

"What about means? Where's the gun, Bobby? Does Kenilworth even own a gun the right caliber?"

"Now, you see, Amanda, that's where hunches get separated from police work," he said smugly. "Mr. Hamilton Kenilworth owns enough guns to blast away half the population of Atlanta without reloading. He is a collector of guns. Big guns. Little guns. Dating from as far back as the Civil War."

Amanda was startled by that bit of news, given Kenilworth's earlier claim that he didn't own a gun, but she tried not to show it. Besides, he could have had thousands of collectible guns stashed away in that mansion of his and still not have owned *the* gun. Collectors didn't always shoot the things—

or so she'd been told. "Does he own the gun used to kill Margaret?" she persisted.

"Somebody's checking his inventory list against his collection even as we speak."

"Do you honestly think he'd polish the murder weapon up and put it back on the shelf?"

"Probably not," he agreed. "But I doubt he had time to redo those inventory lists to get it removed. If the right caliber gun is missing, I guarantee you we can get a conviction."

"Even without showing the actual gun in court?" she said doubtfully. "Or proving he had it in his possession in South Carolina?"

"Even without the gun."

Amanda shook her head. "Whatever happened to the concept of reasonable doubt?"

"There won't be a doubt in the jurors' heads," he promised.

He must have caught her expression, because the cocky demeanor promptly disappeared.

"Okay, what?" he asked.

"You act as if you're taking some sort of personal satisfaction in getting Kenilworth. Did you know him? Before this, I mean?"

"I know his type."

Amanda thought of what Kenilworth had said about a certain kind of justice needing to prove it was blind to wealth and position. "You mean rich and powerful?"

"I mean cold, arrogant, and mean."

His flat tone sent a chill down her spine. He grabbed the check, dropped a generous tip on the table, and headed for the cashier.

When Amanda caught up with him, she snatched the check away, paid it and asked, "What's the deal, Bobby? Did you have run-ins with guys like that in school? Did you resent their privileges?"

The deliberately taunting questions seemed to amuse him. "Hell, no. I was one of them, Amanda, honey. I was raised by one cold, arrogant, mean bastard who had enough money to pave the streets of Myrtle Beach in the stuff, if he'd chosen to do so. He didn't. He would have let someone die of starvation on the front steps before he would have parted with a dime."

He leveled a look straight into her eyes. "But that's not what makes me think Hamilton Kenilworth is guilty, if that's what you're thinking. I believe in my gut the man is guilty, because that's what the evidence is telling me. Pure and simple."

Amanda stared right back at him. "Did it ever occur to you, Bobby, *honey*, that Margaret herself had access to those guns in Kenilworth's collection? And that just maybe she'd taken one along to South Carolina for protection? And that just maybe someone who knew that gun was in the house loaded it and used it on her, then tossed it in the goddamn swamp?"

Leaving him to ponder that scenario, she marched off toward her car. It was no wonder Donelli hated it when she jumped to conclusions during her investigations. Listening to Bobby Claypoole doing the same thing just now had been damned irritating.

She was still fuming when she punched out Jenny Lee's home number on the car phone. As soon as her assistant answered, she said, "The Donovan address. Do you have it?"

"Hey, Jenny Lee? How you doing, Jenny Lee?" the younger woman coached.

"Okay, okay. I'm sorry. The address. Do you have it?"

Jenny Lee sighed heavily. "Of course I have it, Amanda. The magazine pays me to do all your scut work." She reeled off the address so fast, Amanda could barely keep up with her.

Her whole put-upon attitude finally penetrated Amanda's own sour mood. "Jenny Lee, what's going on? You sound miffed."

"Miffed?" she retorted indignantly. "I do not sound *miffed*. I sound furious, or at least that's the attitude I'm going for. I'm sick to death of being left behind while you chase around doing all the fun stuff. Half the time you even forget you have an assistant. Then all of a sudden, like now, you want some piddly little phone number or address you can't be bothered to look up yourself and who do you call? Me. I'm a reporter, Amanda. Or at least I could be if you and Oscar stopped treating me like some dingbat receptionist who got promoted on a whim."

"We don't treat you like that. Or at least I don't." She couldn't be quite so emphatic about Oscar. Come to think of it, she wasn't all that sure about herself. Some of what Jenny Lee was saying rang true. "Do I really treat you like that?"

"Sometimes," she said with a sniff. "Oh, just forget it. I'm in a lousy mood and I'm taking it out on you."

Amanda realized she couldn't contend with Jenny Lee's mood and drive at the same time. She pulled to the curb. "What's really going on here?"

Jenny Lee tried to choke back a sob, but the sound was unmistakable.

"Jenny Lee? Come on, now. Talk to me. This doesn't have anything to do with work, does it?"

"It's Larry," she admitted miserably.

Larry Carter was a freelance photographer *Inside Atlanta*

used on occasion. For some time now he and Jenny Lee had been carrying on a torrid affair.

"What about him?"

"He's been offered a job on *National Geographic*. If he took it, he'd be g-g-gone a-a-all the t-t-time. He'd probably even move t-t-to Washington."

Amanda considered the implications. *National Geographic* was a dream assignment for a photographer. The big time. A showcase for work of the highest caliber. For Larry, who was still in his twenties, it was the break of a lifetime. For Jenny Lee it might be the end of her dream of eventually marrying Larry, maybe becoming some sort of globe-trotting journalistic team. Amanda could just imagine the turmoil both of them must be going through. She knew with all her heart that Larry loved Jenny Lee. She also knew he wasn't ready to settle down and get married.

"Have you talked about it?"

"Not really," Jenny Lee said, sounding somewhat calmer. "He's still in Washington. He called right after they made the offer."

"Did he say he was taking it?"

"Of course he's going to take it," she snapped. "He'd be a fool not to."

"Did he say he was taking it?" Amanda persisted.

Jenny Lee sniffed again. "No," she conceded. "He said we'd talk about it when he got home."

"Then don't you think you're getting all worked up over nothing? Maybe he won't take it. Maybe he'll take the job and take you with him."

That suggestion was greeted by silence. Then, "Do you think he might take me?"

Amanda smiled, glad that Jenny Lee couldn't see her face. "He loves you, you jerk."

"Yeah, he does, doesn't he?" Jenny Lee said, sounding more cheerful.

"You gonna be okay now?"

"Yes. I'm going to take a nice old bubble bath, then put on the sexiest nightie I own and show Mr. Larry Carter that he'd be a flat-out fool to leave me behind."

"Go for it," Amanda encouraged. "I'll talk to you in the morning." She hesitated, then added, "And Jenny Lee, we'll talk more about your duties then, too, okay?"

She couldn't be sure if Jenny Lee even heard her. The phone clicked off about the same time. Obviously Jenny Lee was far more intent on salvaging her relationship with Larry tonight than she was in advancing her career.

Relieved that that particular crisis had been averted, at least for the time being, Amanda detoured in the direction of the address Jenny Lee had given her for the Donovans. She wasn't exactly sure why she wanted to see the Donovan manor. Maybe she was just hoping for inspiration. Correct that. What she was really hoping for was an unlocked front door and a piece of critical evidence. Unfortunately, she wasn't sure she'd recognize the latter if she tripped over it.

Turning her car onto the hilly, winding road on which the Donovans lived, Amanda crept along trying to see the addresses. Most were discreetly hidden on posts that had long since been overgrown with ivy. About half a mile up the road, after passing only a handful of huge homes, she found the road clogged with parked cars. There was barely enough room left for her to squeeze her car through.

When she found the entrance to the next house, she noticed that even more cars lined the long driveway. A party, she guessed. Then she noticed the address. The Donovans? What the hell was going on here? Aside from displaying an inordinate lack of taste, Lottie and Gil weren't even supposed to be in the country.

However, Amanda decided with a certain amount of anticipation, maybe it was a wake for their dear friend Margaret. And given the size of the crowd, one more guest would hardly be noticed.

CHAPTER

Eighteen

Though the grounds of the Donovan home sprawled over what seemed like acres, the house itself was modest, at least by comparison to some of the others Amanda had seen since she'd started working on this story. A two-story brick colonial, it had dark green shutters, a dark green front door, and a healthy patch of out-of-control ivy twining its way toward most of the downstairs windows. If lights hadn't been shining brightly from every single window, it would have had a Gothic air about it.

The music helped to dispel the eerie atmosphere as well. Loud and rhythmic, there was no mistaking it for a funeral dirge. In fact, if Amanda wasn't mistaken, it was live, not Memorex, and being performed by a group with a state-of-the-art, concert-caliber speaker system. She guessed they were somewhere out back, although they could have been in the next county and still been within audience range. It was a wonder the neighbors hadn't lodged formal complaints with the cops. Then again, maybe they'd all gone deaf hours ago.

The type of music and the decibel level gave Amanda her first inkling that Lottie and Gil weren't the hosts for this evening's festivities. This party bore all the earmarks of Vanessa Donovan's kind of affair—overdone and tasteless.

On the front steps a couple, twined around each other like a pair of contortionists, confirmed the impression. No one over the age of twenty-three, twenty-five tops, could get their bodies to do that without risking permanent back injury.

After observing them for a minute just to be sure they weren't engaging in moves she could try on her husband, Amanda strolled through the front door and into the Donovan home. Not one single person she passed along the way seemed to notice her. Judging from the number of beer cans tossed around and the faint, sweet haze of marijuana, it wasn't surprising.

Although she was grateful for the opportunity which had unexpectedly been handed to her, Amanda felt a little like a voyeur as she moved from room to room, ignoring the guests, but hunting diligently for insights into the Donovans. If there were any clues in the house, they weren't likely to be in plain sight, however. She needed to find a den or office, someplace where Gil Donovan was likely to keep financial records, business files, anything that might indicate shady behavior. Hell, she would settle for a stray box of condoms, suspiciously far from the bedroom. Maybe in an expensive leather briefcase, also filled with incriminating paperwork. Now, that would be a treasure worth discovering.

At the end of the formal dining room, she paused just inside a set of French doors to watch the crowd outside dancing to music that hadn't once slowed down since her arrival. The feverish gyrations reminded her one more time that she was getting old. Give her a nice, slow waltz any day. Of course, there were other, more provocative advantages to slow dances that this crowd had apparently not yet discovered. She suddenly realized that she and Donelli had never been on a dance floor. She resolved then and there to check out his sense of rhythm, preferably in their own house so the bedroom wouldn't be too far away.

Intrigued by that plan and anxious to get home and put it into action, she got busy again. Satisfied that the guests here were pretty well occupied outside, she crept upstairs and poked her head in room after room. Fortunately, most were empty, though there was one couple making enthusiastic use of the king-size bed in what appeared to be the master suite. She doubted it was the Donovans, unless they had far fewer inhibitions about getting caught making love by wandering strangers than most middle-aged people she knew.

She finally found an office in a small, windowless room at the end of the upstairs hall. With its tiny bathroom attached, the room had probably once been the maid's quarters. Now the walls were lined with bookshelves and file cabinets. The desk was neat as a pin. Not so much as a paper clip had been left on the smooth pecan surface.

Amanda tugged open the desk drawers. The most exciting thing she found was a mug filled with what had to be disgustingly stale Valentine candies and still wrapped in its bright red cellophane packaging. If it had once had a card with it, that had long since disappeared.

The file cabinets looked more promising. They also seemed to be locked. Bobby Claypoole still had her picklocks, tools he wasn't likely to return anytime soon. Amanda considered trying her luck with a bobby pin, if she had one in the bottom of her purse, or a bent paper clip, if she could find one.

She was about to go back for another search through the

desk for a stray paper clip, when a man inquired softly, "Looking for something?"

There was a lethal sort of calm to the voice that made her turn very slowly until she was face-to-face with its owner, the first person she'd seen since entering the house who appeared to be over thirty. In fact, he looked to be closer to forty, with just a touch of gray in his short blond hair and a round baby face that had been weathered by time and a little too much sun. Probably attained quite recently while on some yacht, she decided with a sinking feeling in the pit of her stomach.

"Mr. Donovan," she guessed.

He nodded.

"Terrific. I've been waiting for you," she said, trying to brazen it out.

He laughed. "Oh, really. Who sent you up here?"

"Vanessa. She told me you were expected home soon."

"Really? If Vanessa had known we were coming home tonight, I guarantee you she would not have allowed her friends to overrun the place. Lottie's downstairs now clearing them out."

Amanda shrugged. "Maybe I misunderstood."

"It happens," he agreed, and waited, clearly fascinated to see what tale she'd spin next.

"Okay, I'll be honest here. I've been trying to reach you for the past couple of days. I drove by tonight, saw all the cars, and guessed you were back from your trip. So here I am."

He nodded. "Plausible . . . up to a point."

She felt as if he'd given her a patronizing pat on the head. She really hated people who did that. Gil Donovan was stacking up to be a more than even match for his hateful wife.

Unfortunately, Amanda was in no position to take him to task for it. She figured she was already treading on very thin ice, if he wanted to get testy about her presence up here. The Atlanta PD, Oscar, Donelli, hell, practically everyone she knew took a dim view of what she liked to think of as her aggressive reporting technique. Some of them actually viewed it as unlawful entry.

Donovan gestured toward a chair, then took the one next to it. "You're the woman from that magazine, right? The one who hassled my wife at the country club."

"I wouldn't put it exactly that way, but we did meet there, yes."

He closed his eyes and rubbed his forehead.

"Headache?" Amanda inquired.

"Too much sun," he confirmed. "Once we heard about Margaret, we turned the yacht around and headed straight back. It's been a long day." He sighed. "I can't believe she's gone, you know. I'm not sure I will believe it until I see her for myself."

"You were very close, weren't you?" At his quizzical expression, she added, "I mean all of you, Lottie, Hamilton, Margaret, and you."

"Yes."

"Was there more? Between you and Margaret?"

A faint smile curved his lips. "Direct, aren't you?"

"I find it saves time."

"And I'm too exhausted to play games with you. Margaret and I did have a brief affair. It was over months ago."

"Whose decision?"

He looked insulted that she would think anyone would turn him out. "Mine," he said, just to emphasize the point.

"Why?"

"I was bored."

"Exactly when did you break it off?"

"I didn't mark the date on my calendar. It wasn't that important."

"Give me your best guess."

"June sometime. Around the middle of the month."

Just about the same time Tommy Ray Baldwin got out of prison, Amanda thought. She doubted Margaret had been too broken up about losing Donovan, if he was telling the truth about calling off their affair. She'd already had her replacement in her sights.

"Were you aware at the time that Margaret's old college sweetheart, a guy named Tommy Ray Baldwin, had just been released from prison?"

"Who?"

He did a credible job of looking blank, so credible that she couldn't be absolutely certain whether he was lying or not. "Never mind. When was the last time you saw Margaret?"

"Last weekend. Sunday night. I spent the weekend finishing up some work at the office."

"The night before she was killed? You're sure about that?"

"Absolutely. Lottie and I left our car at her house. Margaret drove us to the marina."

Odd, Amanda thought. Lauren had mentioned Lottie being in the house the next night, the actual night of the murder. She'd never mentioned Gil being there at all. Had Gil and his wife worked out an agreed-upon alibi for themselves, knowing they'd be likely suspects?

"Which marina?"

"The Blue Dock."

"How did you happen to know about that house?" Amanda wondered, quickly trying to reassemble the puzzle pieces she had been so certain fit another way. "I was under the impression that she had kept it a secret."

"She kept it a secret from Hamilton, not from her lovers."

Amanda was startled by his cool declaration. "There were others?"

"I'm sure," he said, again as if it were a matter of no importance. "Margaret was a woman of insatiable sexual appetites. At the same time, there was a sort of naïveté about her. She always honestly believed that she was in love with whoever happened to be sharing her bed."

"Not a very flattering picture of a woman you once had an affair with."

"An honest one," he countered. "I was never blind to the truth of what we shared."

"Sex?"

"Revenge," he said matter-of-factly. "We were both getting back at Hamilton. The funny thing is, he didn't really give a damn."

"Why was Margaret trying to get even with her husband?"

"Because he ignored her."

"And you? What did you have against him? I thought he was your best friend."

"He was once. Then he met Margaret. She and I were supposed to get married in a month."

Amanda was taken aback once more. "You replaced the man her parents disapproved of so strenuously? I thought Hamilton came along then."

"No, he came next. Instead of marrying me, she ran off with Hamilton."

"And you settled for her best friend?" Amanda said, hating the way these people had used and abused each other.

He didn't answer, but for the first time he looked directly at Amanda. She realized that while Gil Donovan was physically in the room with her, he wasn't there in any way that mattered. His eyes were empty. She found that more chilling than Hamilton Kenilworth's icy demeanor had ever been.

After her encounter with Gil Donovan, Amanda managed to evade Lottie Donovan on her way out. She could hardly wait to get home to Donelli and Pete. She wanted to get warm again, the kind of warmth that came from being loved and needed. She was beginning to wonder if any of the people she'd been interviewing had ever experienced that kind of attachment to another human being. Oddly, Hamilton Kenilworth's relationship with his daughter seemed to come closest. And even there, she couldn't be absolutely sure that he wasn't using the child as some sort of pawn.

Damn. She had never had a longer list of less likable suspects. Kenilworth, Baldwin, and the Donovans. If Margaret had had other lovers, maybe the list was even longer. She supposed all could be said to have a motive for wanting Margaret dead. All had opportunity. Tommy Ray's alibi was shaky and she had only Gil Donovan's word that he'd taken his boat out on Sunday, rather than the beginning of the week, after either he or Lottie had killed Margaret.

It was closer to midnight than she'd realized when she finally got home. Pete was in bed, but Donelli was waiting up for her. At least he'd tried. He was slouched down in his favorite chair, a book open in his lap.

Amanda gently removed the book and settled herself where it had been. A sleepy smile spread across his face even before his eyes came open. "Hey, you," he murmured, cupping her face with his callused hands and bringing her head down until their lips touched.

This, she thought, as the kiss went on and the heat swirled through her, this was what she had come home for.

C H A P T E R

Nineteen

An hour later, settled in bed against a stack of pillows next to her husband and sharing a bowl of rocky road ice cream with him, Amanda couldn't help speculating about the murder. It was one of Donelli's best traits that he didn't hold her one-track mind against her. Maybe that was because for years he'd been on that same track himself and understood the obsessiveness required.

"So what do you think?" she said, passing the bowl back to him for the last spoonful.

"I think the answers are in Myrtle Beach."

"But most of the viable suspects are right here," she argued.

"Now," he said pointedly. "But the scene of the crime is there, whatever hard evidence exists is there, and the suspects' alibis can only be checked out there."

Amanda knew he was right, but for once she was reluctant to leave home. Briefly she considered sending Jenny Lee, but that was no answer. She couldn't leave follow-up this important in her assistant's hands, no matter how desperately Jenny Lee wanted the opportunity to prove herself.

"Damn. This is such a lousy time for me to be away. Pete needs both of us right now."

"Pete is going to be just fine," Donelli reassured her. "We had a long talk today. He didn't tell me where he was from exactly, but he did tell me a little more about what his life was like. He said he'd told you some things, too."

Amanda nodded. "Enough. So what are we going to do?"

"Maybe we should talk to a lawyer and find out what our options are."

"He's just going to say we have to contact the parents, isn't he?"

"Probably," he admitted.

"And what will happen to Pete if we can't keep our promise that he won't ever have to go back home?"

Donelli sighed and pulled her into his arms. "God, what a mess," he murmured.

He shut off the bedside light, casting the room in moon-streaked shadows. The somber conversation took a little of the romance out of the moment, though.

Just then Pete's scream split the silent country night. Racing across the hall, Amanda and Joe found him sitting up in bed, shaking like a leaf, with sweat pouring down his face. They sat on either side of him, quietly reassuring him, but not daring to touch him. A shudder raced through him as his eyes finally came into focus. He moved instinctively into Joe's arms like a small child seeking shelter.

Relieved that the crisis had apparently been nothing more than a bad dream and guessing that Pete might say more about it if she weren't in the room, Amanda pressed a kiss to his brow and left.

It seemed like hours before Joe finally returned to their bed, looking shaken.

"What?" Amanda said.

"He told me about everything," he said grimly. "We're going to see a lawyer and a psychologist in the morning. What his mother subjected him to, what she allowed to happen to him in their own home . . ." He shuddered. "My God, Amanda, how can a parent do such terrible things to a child?"

He didn't need to elaborate for Amanda to deduce that Pete's childhood had been even more grim than she'd feared.

"We'll make it up to him," she vowed. "We'll do whatever it takes to make it up to him."

Over breakfast Amanda's heart ached because Pete refused to meet her eyes. He acted as if he were ashamed, as if he regretted that she knew the ugly truth about his past and feared that she would never look at him again in the same way.

"Joe probably told you stuff, huh?" he said, mashing his cornflakes into a sodden mess.

"Not really," she reassured him. "But Pete, it wouldn't matter if he had. I've told you before, we both love you. Nothing will ever change that. And whatever happened, it wasn't your fault."

She noticed that his eyes remained downcast. "Pete, look at me." When he did, she said again, "It was not your fault."

"You really still want me to be your kid even after . . .?"

"Absolutely," she said emphatically, and saw the sheen of tears spring up in his eyes. "We'll work it out. I promise. No one will ever hurt you again."

"Joe says you're going back to South Carolina."

"For a couple of days."

He regarded her wistfully. "Can I come, too? We made a pretty good team."

"We made a great team. But you need to stay here and get started with the lawyer and the psychologist. That's the most important thing you can do right now."

He sighed. "I suppose," he agreed reluctantly. "How's that kid? Is she okay? Was she there when her mom got killed?"

"I don't think so. She doesn't seem to remember it and her father swears that Margaret was alive when they left."

"You gonna see that police guy again?"

"Probably."

"What about that Baldwin, the guy at the factory?"

"Probably."

He scowled at her. "I don't like it. Maybe me and Joe better come along. We can do this other stuff later."

. "Sorry, kiddo. This time I have to work alone. I'll call every day and tell you what's happening, okay? You can give me your advice."

He didn't seem pleased by the offer. "Yeah, right, and who's going to look out for you over there? The cop?"

Amanda grinned at him. "Here's the first lesson you need to learn if you're going to be my son. I don't need anybody to look after me. I can take care of myself."

Pete rolled his eyes. "Yeah, right."

She gathered up her briefcase and overnight bag, then gave him a kiss on the cheek as she passed by. "Work on that attitude, pal. This is the nineties. Women don't need men to rescue them. You'll save yourself a lot of grief later, if you learn that now."

"Maybe you don't need to be rescued," he shot back. "But Joe says sometimes you need a keeper."

Amanda was glad Bobby Claypoole wasn't around to hear that. She'd have to take back her previous night's testimonial about Donelli's liberated attitude.

The first thing she did when she arrived back in Myrtle Beach a few hours later was return to Margaret's oceanfront house. She parked in the driveway, which was empty now that the Donovans had removed their car. A streetlamp down the block didn't shed much light on the property, but the moon was just about full. There was no mistaking the band of yellow tape the police had left across the front of the house. It didn't matter. She hadn't intended to go inside anyway.

While she sat there, breathing in the salty air and listening to the distant crash of waves, Amanda tried to visualize again how things must have happened the night of the murder. She had a different scenario for each of the likely suspects.

For instance, had Margaret followed her husband through the house as he reclaimed his daughter? Amanda could practically hear their shouts, could feel Margaret's anguish as Hamilton gathered up Lauren and her belongings and took them to his waiting rental car. The front door would have been standing open for the trips back and forth, allowing neighbors to hear, but not necessarily to see the fight. Had the argument escalated? Had it become so violent and filled with threats that Kenilworth had returned one last time and shot his wife to avoid a nasty custody battle?

Try as she might, Amanda just couldn't see the cool, distant lawyer she knew losing control of his temper. He struck her as the kind of man whose angriest responses would be cold and carefully calculated, which meant the murder if he had committed it would most likely have been premeditated. Once again she thought, would he ever have done such a thing in front of his child? She didn't think so.

Okay, then, if Margaret had been alive when her husband and child left, was it possible that Baldwin had slipped home from work? Maybe he had overheard part of the argument, feared that Margaret was going to return to her husband after all because of Lauren, and shot her rather than lose her.

It was an interesting scenario. Envisioning it reminded Amanda that she had no idea how Baldwin had gotten to work that night. Pete hadn't found Margaret's rental car at the factory and there had been no other car in the driveway earlier in the evening, suggesting that Tommy Ray didn't have a car of his own, even though he had instinctively reached for keys when she'd been with him at the factory. She made a note to check for bus schedules and taxi records on the night of the murder. She also needed to find out what had happened to that rental car.

Next, Lottie and Gil Donovan. She doubted they would have committed the murder together, which meant that perhaps they had come to Myrtle Beach separately. Maybe Lottie had driven over, visited with Margaret, Baldwin, and Lauren. Maybe she'd even been in the house when Hamilton took his daughter away. With Baldwin at work and Lauren gone, maybe then she had confronted Margaret about her affair with Gil and, in a jealous rage, shot her, then gone to the marina to wait for her husband. Amanda could buy all of that.

Finally, there was Gil. Perhaps he had flown into town late that night and come to the house expecting to share a bed with Margaret before taking off on his trip with his wife the next day. Perhaps Margaret had turned him away, declared that the affair was over, that she was in love with Baldwin. Then Donovan, stung by the rejection, might have shot her, then joined Lottie at the marina.

They all had nice, tidy explanations for their activities that night. One of them had to be lying, but which one? She simply couldn't be sure. Sitting there in the driveway, absorbing the atmosphere, Amanda found that all but one of the scenarios played out believably. That meant that discovering the detailed movements of those three suspects should give her a picture of what had really happened the night of the murder. She would leave Kenilworth for last, in case none of those other three panned out and she was forced to consider him the prime suspect.

Satisfied that there was nothing more to be learned by sitting outside the house, and seeing no reason to risk Bobby Claypoole's wrath by breaching the yellow crime scene tape, Amanda pulled out of the driveway and headed for a pay phone to look up the address of the local taxi company.

Unfortunately, there were several. She called for directions to the offices of the closest one to the house, assuming that would be the one anyone leaving Margaret's would call. She hoped she'd find the information she needed the first time out, without having to visit every taxi dispatcher in town.

After several wrong turns in a seedy area of town, she finally found the dispatch center tucked away southwest of the downtown tourist area. After pressing a bell and identifying herself, she waited several seconds before the door was finally buzzed open.

Inside, she found a two-person control center. One woman, who identified herself as Dottie, was taking incoming requests for taxis, while another was handling the dispatching. There was a fair amount of joking over the airwaves amid the requests for exact directions, descriptions of the clients to be picked up, and the occasional question about flat rates for certain trips. The two women handled the resulting chaos with amazing aplomb.

It was the gray-haired, sweet-talking Dottie who finally turned her full attention on Amanda. The phones had stopped ringing, but the radio chatter was incessant.

"You say you're from a magazine over in Atlanta?" Dottie asked.

"That's right. I'm doing a story on the murder of Margaret Clayton Kenilworth."

She clicked her tongue. "Wasn't that just the most awful thing? That poor baby of hers. Who's going to look after her with her mama dead and her daddy in jail?"

"I've been worried about that, too," Amanda confessed. "I guess that's why I'm so anxious to see if I can find some information that would prove the father didn't do it. I was wondering if I could get a look at your taxi records for that night, see if you had some pick-ups or drop-offs at that address. I'm also wondering about any fares that might have been taken to the Blue Dock Marina."

A flurry of incoming calls kept the woman from answering, but the younger woman on dispatch, who'd apparently filtered out the radio activity to hear most of what Amanda had said, gestured toward a file cabinet. "Everything's in there. Filed by date. All the sheets for that night should be in the same folder. Help yourself. If you'd like a cup of coffee, there's a fresh pot. Just check the mugs, though. The guys on the earlier shift don't wash 'em out half the time."

"Thanks." Amanda found a clean mug, poured herself some black coffee just about the consistency of mud. Apparently they liked it strong, she thought as the first sip sent a shudder through her. She figured that one jolt would keep her up the rest of the night. At the snail's pace at which this investigation was proceeding, she figured that was a good thing.

It didn't take long to locate the file for the night of the murder. Someone believed in tidy records. Removing the file from the drawer, she went through it page by page.

It had been a busy night. It seemed to take forever, but she finally found an entry at 10:43 P.M., a pick-up at Margaret's house with a drop-off at the T-shirt factory. Hard as she looked, though, she couldn't find another one indicating Baldwin had come back to the house that night, at least not by taxi.

Noticing that there was another lull in calls, she asked Dottie, "Do you have any idea if there's a bus route between the scene of the murder and the T-shirt factory out on the highway?"

"Sure," she said. "But it would mean a transfer and at that time of night, it would take forever. The bus schedule slows way down after rush hour."

So, for the moment, anyway, that seemed to let Tommy Ray Baldwin off the hook. He would have had to borrow a car from the only other man on duty at the factory that night and the police would surely have learned about that by now, if it had happened. Amanda went back to the taxi records to see if any trips had been made between the airport and the house or the house and the marina. She couldn't find a damn one.

Frustrated, she finished her coffee, then put the file away. "Thanks for your help."

"Did you find anything?"

She shook her head. "Nothing. I'm heading to the marina now."

"Talk to Jake Webster over there. Tell him Dottie Hastings sent you," the gray-haired woman said. "Jake's drunk half the time, but he don't miss much and he keeps damned good records to remind him of things."

Perfect, Amanda thought as she drove toward the marina. She just loved compulsive people. She could hardly wait to get her hands on Jake Webster's observations about the Donovans. She didn't care how soused the man was, as long as he'd put what he'd seen in writing. It made it so much nicer when it came time to go to court.

CHAPTER

Twenty

While she was on her way to meet Jake Webster, Amanda realized that she had once again left Jenny Lee back in Atlanta with nothing to do. She wouldn't be surprised to find that her assistant had quit the minute she realized Amanda had taken off without her and left no instructions behind. She dialed the *Inside Atlanta* number and asked for Jenny Lee. Oscar took the call, snapping out a greeting. It was not a good sign, she decided.

"Where's Jenny Lee?" she inquired warily.

"Home would be my guess," he told her. "She took off out of here this morning, slamming every door between my office and the elevator. She seems to think we're not taking advantage of her skills."

"We're not," Amanda agreed. "Did she quit?"

"Not exactly. She said something to the effect that when we found something for her to do, we could damn well call her. Meantime, she had closets that needed cleaning."

Amanda bit back a chuckle. Somehow it seemed to be

inappropriate to be laughing when Jenny Lee was so clearly miserable. "I'll call her."

"I'd like to point out that you were the one who begged for an assistant," Oscar said. "You told me how much more you could accomplish with someone to do your legwork. You carried on until I said Jenny Lee could have the job. You got what you wanted, Amanda. Now you'd damn well better start to use her. I'm not paying somebody to stay at home and clean closets."

"Of course not. I'll take care of it," she reassured him. "I have something for her to do right now, as a matter of fact."

"What?"

She'd been afraid he was going to ask that. She jumped on the first thought that came to mind. "I want her to interview the Claytons again. I'm getting a real bad impression of their daughter from the suspects in the case. I need another perspective."

"Good idea. You figured out who did it yet?"

"The police arrested Kenilworth," she pointed out.

"What kind of idiot do you think I am, Amanda? Obviously you don't believe they have the right guy or you'd be in here now writing your story, instead of gallivanting all over the South hunting down more evidence and making me crazy wondering if you'll meet your damned deadline, which by the way is the day after tomorrow."

"I'll meet it. I'll wrap this up, then write all night if I have to," she said with more confidence than was probably justified. "Gotta go. I want to catch Jenny Lee and get her back to work."

Jenny Lee was, indeed, rearranging her closets. Had been all day, she said. She pointedly proclaimed it to be the most satisfying work she had done in a long time. She refused to discuss Larry at all, which suggested that their reunion had not gone terribly well.

"I guess you're too busy, then, to do an interview for me," Amanda said.

"What interview?" Jenny Lee asked suspiciously.

"Margaret's parents."

"You're kidding," she said, her voice brightening considerably. "You want me to go see the Claytons?"

"You were with me before. That'll probably make Mrs. Clayton more willing to talk, since she'll remember you. Besides, you talk her language."

"English?" Jenny Lee said, sounding thoroughly puzzled.

"Southern," Amanda corrected. That, thank goodness, drew a laugh.

"Okay, I suppose I can do that," Jenny Lee relented. "What am I after?"

"We need to know more about Margaret. I'm getting a lot of garbage from the men in her life indicating she was some sort of nymphomaniac."

Jenny Lee gasped. "Amanda, I can't ask her mother that!"

"No, of course not. Just see if they were worried about her relationships with men. They obviously didn't much like Tommy Ray when he and Margaret dated in college. Gil says he was dating her before Hamilton came into the picture and stole her. He claims his affair was revenge on Kenilworth for stealing her away. See if any of that tracks with what the parents remember. Get their impressions of Gil. It seems odd to me that Mrs. Clayton didn't even mention him when we were there the first time, particularly if they thought he and Margaret were well suited for each other."

"Got it."

Amanda recalled the impromptu scenario she'd tossed at

Bobby Claypoole the night before. It bore checking out. "Oh, and one last thing. See if Margaret ever carried a gun for protection and if so, what kind it was. If they don't know, maybe Jim Harrison can see if she had a gun registered."

"Got it. Anything else?"

"Just one thing," she said, shifting to a gentler, more personal tone. "Whatever's happening with Larry right now, you'll work it out. I really believe that."

Jenny Lee sighed. "I surely do hope so, Amanda. I'd hate to have to wreck all his Atlanta Braves memorabilia."

When the phone clicked in her ear, Amanda was still chuckling over Jenny Lee's notion of suitable retaliation for a broken heart. She was right, though. Not much would hurt Larry worse than losing his beloved collection of Braves' mementos.

Amanda found the man she assumed was Jake Webster beside a shack on the back side of the marina's parking lot. He was lounging in a decrepit lawn chair, an unidentifiable bottle in his hand, his gaze directed seaward. When she called out to him, he rose with surprising alacrity and came to meet her.

His hair was nearly all white, his skin a leathery brown. He was a little bowlegged and walked with the rolling gait of a seaman, as if he expected the deck to be shifting under his feet at any second. His black T-shirt strained across a wide chest and was tucked into a pair of belted jeans that looked as if they'd suffered one too many dunkings in the ocean. They were faded to the muted shade of blue sea-glass.

"I'm Jake," he said, as if she might not have guessed that by his quick response to her shout. "What can I do for you?"

"Dottie Hastings said you might be able to help me find some information I need."

His prompt, wicked grin suggested Jake must have been

quite a rake in his time and that his memories of Dottie were purely indecent. Hell, maybe they weren't memories. Amanda had noticed him giving her an appreciative once-over as he'd approached. Jake looked to be in his seventies. That didn't mean his libido was dead. And despite that bottle he'd discreetly left over by his chair, he also appeared sober.

"What might you be needing?"

Amanda tried to place the accent and couldn't. Irish? Scottish? With a touch of South Carolina mixed in?

"Actually I was wondering if you could point out the Donovan yacht."

"Why would you be needing to see that?"

So, she thought, for all of his jovial, helpful manner, Jake Webster knew exactly who paid his salary. It wasn't Amanda. It wasn't even his friend Dottie Hastings. Amanda pulled a business card from her purse and handed it to him as she explained the story she was working on.

"The Donovans said they were out on their boat at the time of the murder. I was hoping to confirm that. I also figured a look at the boat might come in handy when I sit down to write the article."

"I suppose looking won't hurt nothing," he decided eventually. "This way. Can't let you on board, you understand, but you can get a pretty good idea what it's like from the outside."

He led her along a gray, weathered dock that appeared to be in excellent repair. The boats in the slips closest to shore were smaller, but even they were hardly rowboats. Amanda guessed that most had berths and galleys belowdecks, if not even more elaborate living quarters. Still, she couldn't help an expression of openmouthed astonishment when they reached the end of the dock and Jake said, "There she is. A beauty, isn't she?"

She was a beauty, all right. About a million dollars worth, Amanda guessed. Maybe more, depending on just how far the brass and teak fittings extended inside and how much a decorator had been paid to do the cabins. Jake looked pretty smug about her expression of astonishment.

"How many people does this hold?" she asked, trying to keep a note of awe out of her voice. She swore to herself that she did not envy the way the other half lived. Right at this moment, though, she figured she was lying to herself. She would definitely like to have a fancy yacht like this in her life and the time to cruise it, say in the Mediterranean.

"Twenty, twenty-four," he said. "Depends on how friendly they are. Plus the crew, of course. The Donovans take a captain, a steward, and a chef along when they're entertaining guests."

"Of course," Amanda said dryly. "So, did they take it out recently?"

"Sure did. Just her and him this time. Said they needed a little getaway all to themselves. Came back mighty fast, though. I could tell there was trouble right off. It's not like them to cut short a trip like that. When they go, they pretty much cut themselves off from their cares."

"How did they seem when they left?"

"Tired, I suppose you'd say. A little stressed out, but then that's usually why they want to take the boat out in the first place, to relax."

"Did they arrive together?"

He hesitated. "Now let me think on that a minute. I recall seeing her early in the day, maybe about noon. Didn't see him till later. Of course, that was pretty much the way they always showed up. She'd come early to stock up on supplies.

He'd come after work, I suppose. They'd leave the next morning before dawn."

"I understand they didn't have their car here with them. Do you recall how they arrived?"

"Let me see, now. Mrs. Donovan, she showed up with another lady. Right pretty little thing. Had a girl with them, too. Maybe about six, seven years old. Blond. They didn't go on the boat. Just said good-bye right in the parking lot."

Okay, then, Margaret and Lauren had dropped off Lottie, Amanda concluded. "What about Mr. Donovan? How did he get here?"

"You know, now that I think back on it, I don't believe I saw him arrive this time. I'd gone out to have a drink or two with a friend. When I got back, 'round about midnight, maybe one in the morning, it was the guard on duty who told me Mr. Donovan was here."

"Which means he got here between, what? Six or seven in the evening and one A.M.?"

Webster nodded. "That'd be about right. Can't say for sure. I could call the other fellow for you. He might recall."

"Would you? That would be great."

They walked back to the weatherbeaten shack. Inside, it was neat as a pin. It also turned out to be Jake's quarters, not the marina office as she had guessed. "I thought this was the office."

He laughed. "Hell, no. That big fancy building up on the road is the office and club room. Has a high-priced restaurant inside, too. They give me this room down here in exchange for keeping an eye on the place."

"So you can't check the records for me?"

He grinned. "You want their records or mine? Keep my

own logs right here. Don't want somebody coming in and saying this or that happened and me not being able to prove it didn't.'' He pulled an old, leather-bound volume out from under his bed. He patted the binding. ''It's all right here. Which boats came and went, who took them out, when they got back, strangers visiting, just about anything you might be needing to know.''

''Then you can check on the exact date the Donovans went out?''

''You bet,'' he said, flipping the volume open and running a gnarled finger down a column of neat notations. ''Here 'tis. Monday a week ago. They left at five-twenty A.M.''

Just hours after Margaret was killed, Amanda thought triumphantly. And though Jake had seen Lottie get on that boat in the afternoon the day before, it was certainly possible she'd left again between then and 5:20 the next morning. She was still a viable suspect in Amanda's book.

''Now let me call old Earl and see if he recalls how Mr. Donovan got here the night before and what time he came in,'' Webster said.

While he was on the phone, Amanda glanced around the tiny quarters that he'd turned into a cheerful, if somewhat spartan home. His single bed was made with military precision. She was sure a coin would have bounced on the sheets. A stack of books rested on a bedside table and more sat on the floor. A tiny refrigerator, a hotplate, and a pint-sized microwave made up a kitchen in one corner of the room. A television sat on an upturned crate with the room's only chair in front of it. An open door on the left revealed a toilet and sink, but there was no room for anything more. Maybe he had shower privileges up at the main building.

''Of course,'' he said gleefully, slapping his thigh as he

listened to Earl. "I shoulda recollected that. Now, don't you go forgetting that I'm taking the night off on Thursday this week. Don't be late, neither. I've got a date with the prettiest little gal this side of Killarney."

Amanda waited for him to share the news that he was fairly bursting to convey.

"Don't know why I didn't think of this," he told her with a rueful shake of his head. "Just shows what happens when I don't put it down in my book."

"What?"

"The car. Why, it sat right out there in the parking lot the whole time the Donovans were gone."

"What car?"

"White, I believe it was. A rental. Struck me as odd, since I'd never before knowed him to rent a car, not just to leave it sitting in the parking lot. Mr. Donovan always struck me as a little too tight with a buck to do something like that."

Exhilaration raced through Amanda. Margaret's missing rental car had been white. If that was the car that had sat here for several days, then it placed Gil Donovan at her house sometime on the night of the murder—after Amanda had driven by that first night with Pete and before Donovan had left port the next morning.

"Any record of the license number?" she asked, hardly daring to hope that it would be written down, since Jake had clearly forgotten all about it.

He grinned at her. "Does a dog have fleas? Got it right here." He pulled out a folded-up piece of paper which had been stuck in the back of his logbook. "Keep a list a tag numbers, just in case."

"In case of what?" Amanda wondered.

"In case something turns up missing around here. I can

check my list against the cars registered by the marina's regular clients and identify any that didn't belong here. Never know when that might lead to some crook who stopped by to get into mischief." He handed her the list. "You know what you're looking for?"

She nodded and extracted the tag numbers Pete had jotted down at Margaret's house that first night they were in town. She found a match halfway down Jake Webster's list. "Bingo," she said triumphantly. "Now, what do you suppose Gil Donovan was doing with the murder victim's car?"

Jake's eyes brightened with interest. "You mean to say there might be a real connection between Mr. Donovan and that murder?"

Amanda grinned at him. "You bet there is, and thanks to you, I can prove it."

"Well, I'll be damned. That'll teach folks around here to make fun of all my little notes."

"Can you make me a copy of that sheet? You'd better hang on to the original in case the police want it."

"Sure can. It'll take me a minute to get to the main building and run one off on the copier. You mind waiting?"

"For this? Absolutely not. I'll just have a seat outside and breathe in some of that tangy salt air."

Sitting in that old lawn chair of Webster's, Amanda could see why a man might be content with just the basics in life and not much else. It was awfully peaceful down here with just the moon and stars and the occasional chug of a boat's motor for company.

When the old man came back with her copy, Amanda thanked him again for his help. "You hang on to that list of yours, now. I have a feeling the police are definitely going to want a look at it."

In fact, she decided as she got back into her car, this little piece of information might be her gift to Bobby Claypoole. She figured she'd better pass it along before he tossed Hamilton Kenilworth into a cell and threw away the key.

CHAPTER
Twenty-one

Maybe the conversation with Bobby Claypoole could wait until morning, Amanda decided, reneging on her rare burst of generosity. If Kenilworth hated being in jail all that much, he would have fought harder to keep from being sent there. Since where he spent the night apparently didn't matter to him, she might as well take a little longer to work the story's angles to be absolutely sure of what she had before she shared her information with the police.

One thing troubled her about the noose that seemed to be tightening around Gil Donovan's neck. Why would a very smart attorney drive the victim's car anywhere, much less leave it where it could be easily traced to him? Sure, there were theories about hiding things in plain sight, but evidence in a murder case?

And where was the car now? Had he blithely turned it in at the airport? Why not do that first thing, if he'd merely needed a car to get away from the house after murdering Margaret? He could have dropped it off using one of those speedy check-in systems which didn't require the driver to speak to a soul. The rental company would never have known who'd brought it back.

Then Donovan could have taken a shuttle to the terminal and caught a cab for the marina. The car would have been cleaned up and put back in the fleet before the police could trace it. Very tidy, a hell of a lot tidier than parking it in the marina lot for days on end.

Unless, she was forced to admit, Gil Donovan had nothing to hide. Maybe Margaret had planned to go back to her husband and simply told Gil he might as well use the car and turn it in after his trip. No, she decided, that made no sense. If he needed a car, why not just take Lottie's? Because that would be an admission that he'd been to see Margaret? But wouldn't driving Margaret's rental car have been suspect as well?

Amanda muttered a curse under her breath. This was getting too damned complicated. The whole car thing was crazy. She flipped through her notebook, found the Donovans' phone number, and dialed.

"Yes, what?" Gil Donovan asked, sounding cranky and half asleep.

"Sorry if I woke you," Amanda said. "I need to ask you a question about the night you arrived in Myrtle Beach."

"Who the hell is this?"

"Amanda Roberts."

Her name apparently stunned him, because it took him forever to respond. Finally he said, "Call me in the morning at the office."

"It won't take long."

"In the morning," he snapped, and hung up.

Definitely not a night person, Amanda decided as she

returned to the same beachfront hotel where she and Pete had stayed a few nights before. It seemed like eons ago. Thinking of it reminded her that she'd meant to call home to see how the meetings with the attorney and the psychologist had gone. She glanced at her watch. It was nearly eleven, which might as well have been the middle of the night as far as a farmer was concerned. Even though Joe wasn't up at dawn tending fields at this time of the year, he tended to keep the same hours he did in the summer.

As soon as she'd checked in and gone up to her room, Amanda sat on the edge of the bed and debated calling home anyway. What the hell? If she couldn't wake up her own husband, who could she wake up?

Apparently Donelli wasn't asleep after all, because he snatched the phone up on the first ring.

"I miss you," he said at once.

She laughed and settled back against the pillows. "How'd you know it was me?"

"Who else would risk calling me at this hour? How's it going?"

"I thought I had a break, but now I'm not so sure." She told him about the car. "It seems too obvious, almost like somebody left it there to frame Donovan."

Only after she had formed the thought aloud did Amanda realize that she should have considered that possibility earlier.

"Have you asked him about it?"

"He hung up on me. He told me to call him back in the morning. I guess he doesn't like being awakened out of a sound sleep by a nosy reporter."

"Or he doesn't want to answer questions with his wife listening in," Donelli suggested.

"Under the circumstances, that's probably a valid consideration. I should have thought of it."

"You can't think of everything. That's why you have me."

"I thought I had you for other things."

He laughed. "Those, too."

Amanda sighed. "Joe?"

"Uh-oh, I sense a serious change in mood here."

"How'd it go with Pete today?"

Amanda could hear him shifting position on their bed,
settling in for a talk.

"I spoke to a lawyer in Atlanta, somebody Jim Harrison
recommended, as a matter of fact. He said he'd start checking
to see if Social Services in Pete's hometown have any reports
of abuse on record. He's got a PI doing a background check
on the parents. Once he has that, he'll see if we've got enough
to take into court to get Pete put into our custody."

"Isn't that too important to leave to somebody else? Maybe
you should go check it out yourself."

"I can't. Not while you're away. Somebody has to be here
with Pete. I don't dare take him along with me. It's too risky.
Somebody might spot him and report to his parents. I think
our best bet for getting custody is to take them by surprise.
If I'm not satisfied with what's happening, I'll go myself after
you get home."

"You're okay with waiting?" she asked, listening for signs
of frustration in his voice.

"It's the way it has to be. I'm fine with it."

He sounded as if he meant it, she decided. "You didn't
say last night. Where's Pete from?"

"Pittsburgh. He took all the money he'd saved from odd
jobs and went to the bus station. He only had enough to get

as far south as Atlanta. He wanted to go to Orlando. I guess he figured he'd be safe in a town that caters to kids' dreams with all those amusement parks. Anyway, he'd been here about a month when we met him."

"Did you get him in to see a psychologist?"

"I'm still working on that. The lawyer recommended a guy named Drake. Garrison Drake, I think. The guy must be good. I couldn't get an appointment for another three weeks."

"Is Pete okay with all this?"

"He's not saying too much. I think he's scared. I also think he's just a little excited, but terrified of getting his hopes up. I'm really glad we're doing this, though. His school counselor called today to say the change in him since the start of the school year has been nothing short of miraculous. She thinks he could wind up with straight A's on his report card."

"You're kidding!" she said incredulously. "He never cracks a book."

Donelli laughed. "Amanda, letting us see him studying wouldn't be cool. That doesn't mean he doesn't do it." He hesitated, then asked, "You're still okay with all this, right? No reservations about adopting him?"

"None," she reassured him. She realized to her amazement that she was no longer fearful of becoming a parent, something that had terrified her only a few weeks earlier. In fact, the only thing that scared her now was the possibility that the courts might not allow Pete to remain with them. She wasn't sure she'd be able to bear losing him.

"This bed's lonely without you," Donelli said, pushing thoughts of Pete straight out of her head. His voice had dropped a seductive notch. "Come home soon."

"As soon as I can."

"'Night, Amanda."

"'Night, Joe."

It was several seconds before either of them put the phone back on the hook, as if neither wanted to be the first to break the connection.

At the stroke of nine A.M., Amanda was on the phone to Kenilworth, Kenilworth, James and Donovan. Fortunately, Gil was at his desk and took her call. She did so love a man who was prompt.

"Don't ever call me at home on this stuff again," he snapped the instant he got on the line.

"Things a little tense at home?" Amanda inquired cheerfully. She liked an edgy suspect. They sometimes revealed the most fascinating things they'd meant to keep secret.

"My marriage is none of your concern."

"It is if it has anything to do with Margaret's murder."

"It doesn't. Now what do you want?"

"Let's start with why you lied to me."

"About what?"

"You said you left Myrtle Beach on Sunday. I have evidence it was Monday."

"So I was off a day. I told you I'd been working 'round the clock to get everything cleared off my desk so I could take a vacation. I lost track of time. What's the big deal?"

"The big deal should be obvious. Margaret was killed on Monday. You weren't somewhere in the middle of the Atlantic. You were in Myrtle Beach."

"Okay, I see your point, but I didn't have anything to do with her murder. You'll just have to take my word for it."

"Maybe I will, but the police won't."

"You let me worry about the police. Good-bye."

"Not just yet," Amanda said hurriedly. "How did you get to the marina the night you arrived in Myrtle Beach?"

"What the hell does that have to do with anything?"

"Maybe nothing. Humor me."

"Okay, I drove."

"What?"

"A rental car."

"Margaret's?"

Up until now the responses had been quick and uncensored. The last question, though, seemed to have silenced him. "Well?" she prodded.

"Why the hell would I have had Margaret's car?"

To Amanda's regret, his bemusement actually sounded fairly convincing. "I figured maybe you stopped to pay her a visit and she loaned it to you."

"If I'd been to the house, which I hadn't, and if I had needed a car, which I didn't, why wouldn't I have taken my wife's?"

"Good question."

"Ms. Roberts, you're not making any sense. Why would you connect me with Margaret's rental car?"

"Because it was left in the marina parking lot the same night you arrived. It sat there the whole time you were on your trip. Now it's gone."

"What the hell? You've must have it wrong."

"I don't," she said, though she had to wonder what the hell was going on. His puzzlement sounded genuine. Of course, he'd already lied to her once. There was no reason for him not to try it again.

"Look, I don't know how it got there, but I can damn well

guess why. Somebody wanted to make it look as if I had something to do with Margaret's murder.''

"That would certainly be my guess," Amanda agreed. "Let's run through the options. Your wife. Did she leave the yacht that night after you'd arrived?"

"Not that I know of. I'm a sound sleeper, though. I suppose it's possible."

Amanda was surprised at how readily he'd delivered his wife up as a suspect. He hadn't even hesitated before answering. Obviously he didn't intend to provide her with an airtight alibi, not even when doing so could have assured him of one of his own by accounting for his whereabouts all night.

"How about Baldwin? Did he know about you? Was he aware you were at the marina that night?"

"If I didn't know about him, why would he know about me?"

"Unless Lottie mentioned it while she was at the house earlier. If she had, he could have been jealous of your relationship with Margaret."

"*Prior* relationship," he corrected. "So he had no reason to be jealous."

"How about Kenilworth?" she asked, even though she couldn't imagine that he knew about the marina if he hadn't even known about his wife's house in Myrtle Beach.

"Of course," he said. "That was the sweetest irony, you see. He and Margaret went out with us on the boat on several occasions. She had a house only a few miles away and never once invited him there."

Amanda wasn't wild about the picture she was getting. Kenilworth was cold and arrogant. He was also proud. Once he'd found out about the house and figured out that the Donovans must have known about it, had he killed Margaret and used her car in an attempt to frame Donovan for the crime? God, she hoped not. She couldn't imagine what life would be like for Lauren if she had to grow up with those two sets of warring grandparents.

"What are you up to now?" Donovan asked.

"I'm going to the jail to see Kenilworth and lay this all out for him."

"Careful, Ms. Roberts. Hamilton doesn't like being crossed."

"I'll keep that in mind."

Before taking off to track Kenilworth down at the local jail, where he was no doubt ensconced by now, Amanda called Jenny Lee. "How'd it go with the Claytons?"

"They defended their daughter. They said she might have made a few misjudgments along the way. I gathered that was an understatement, but they refused to elaborate beyond saying about a thousand times that that Tommy Ray Baldwin person—their phrasing—was the creep who just about destroyed her back in college and had probably killed her now."

"That's a familiar refrain," Amanda noted. "How about a gun? Did she own one?"

"Her mama flat-out said no, but her daddy took me aside later and said he'd helped her get some little lady's pistol to protect herself. Said he'd insisted she carry it in her purse, what with all the crazies in the world these days."

"She had a license?"

"Sure did. Right on file with the Atlanta police. All nice and legal. Made Jim Harrison's eyes practically bug out when he found it."

"Thanks, Jenny Lee. You're terrific."

"What should I do now?"

"I'll have to get back to you on that." Amanda hung up slowly.

She couldn't help wondering why Bobby Claypoole hadn't said a peep when she'd painted that scenario about Margaret having a gun in the house. Had he been holding out on her? It wouldn't be the first time a cop had done that. In fact, some of them seemed to delight in keeping her in the dark as much as possible. That was what made it such a pure delight to stay one step ahead of them.

Of course, it was also possible that they hadn't found that gun in Margaret's purse. If they hadn't, where the hell was it? Locked away somewhere in the house, maybe. Or at the bottom of some swamp outside of town, tossed there by the killer.

C H A P T E R

Twenty-two

*S*omething kept nagging at Amanda. She just knew if she could ever figure out exactly what was bothering her, she'd be able to identify the real killer. Maybe one last visit with Tommy Ray Baldwin would help to speed up the process. She didn't believe he was guilty, but she needed reassurance. And there were a few things he might be able to clarify for her.

She drove to the factory and went through the same procedure. Baldwin turned up within minutes. He looked more exhausted than before, but he seemed willing enough to talk. It was hardly the attitude she would have expected from a man who'd killed the woman he'd loved for more than ten years. That accomplished one of her missions. She was reassured.

Once again they went outside and Tommy Ray immediately lit up a cigarette.

"Those things will kill you, you know," Amanda said.

He laughed. "I can read the warnings and I know all about

the research. A man's allowed one vice, though, don't you think? Most of the others aren't allowed in prison."

He looked her over, the appreciative glance of a man who couldn't prevent himself from checking out every woman, no matter her availability or his own. Not even his obvious grief could prevent the automatic behavior.

"So, what's the deal?" he asked. "Why are you back? I thought this case was over."

"I'm just wondering about a couple of loose ends. For instance, how did you get to work the night of the murder?"

"Taxi. My car was here. I'd left it the night before."

That explained his grab for his keys. "Tell me about Margaret's gun."

He shook his head. "That thing," he said with an air of disgust. "I told her all it was going to do was get her killed when some thief turned in on her. She didn't have the guts to use it. She'd have been better off with a can of mace or pepper spray, but she wouldn't listen."

"Did she keep it locked away in the house?"

"Nope. Carried it in her purse, just like her fool of a daddy told her to." He regarded her oddly. "Is that the gun that was used to kill her?"

Amanda shook her head. "I don't know. Describe it for me, though, just in case the police have it as evidence."

"Small, .22-caliber, had a pretty ol' pearl handle. Better for looking at than shooting."

She jotted down the description. It matched the kind of gun a lot of women bought, liking the size and weight without giving a thought to how little damage it could inflict except at very close range.

"One more thing. You mentioned that Kenilworth had a stake in getting Lauren back home. What did you mean?"

"I meant that Margaret would never have gone back to him if she'd had a choice. She wanted to marry me. Lauren was the pawn. If Hamilton took that little girl away, Margaret wasn't about to break up their marriage. She'd have been back home on the next plane."

"That must have infuriated you."

He shook his head. "It just made me sad. We'd already lost a lot of years together. I figured the odds weren't good this time around, either, but I was willing to give it a shot. I should have known Margaret wasn't strong enough or brave enough to fight Kenilworth for her daughter. And face it. The fact was, I was a liability to her. Who'd give custody to a woman living with an ex-con rather than the fine upstanding father, a pillar of the community with endless resources? If I were a judge, I'm not so sure I would."

"How'd you feel about that?"

"Hurt, but realistic. I knew I'd lose her. The only question was when. I figured it was only a matter of time before Kenilworth caught up with her and played his trump card."

Amanda was convinced of the answer, but she had to ask the question one more time. "Did you kill her?"

The question didn't seem to offend him. Again, he just looked tired.

"Why would I do that? I loved her," he said simply. "I always had."

Driving away from her interview with Tommy Ray Baldwin, Amanda thought she finally knew for certain who had killed Margaret Kenilworth. What saddened her, though, was that so many lives had been ripped apart, and all because the Claytons had decided ten years ago that they knew what was best for their daughter. Whether they had deliberately set

Tommy Ray up in that hit-and-run slaying or not, they certainly had done nothing to be supportive of his relationship with their daughter. Maybe if they had, none of this would have been happening now.

She reached once again for her car phone and called Bobby Claypoole.

"You're just in time, Amanda, honey."

"In time for what?"

"We're about to take Hamilton Kenilworth into court to be arraigned on charges of first-degree murder."

"Oh, shit. Bobby, you can't do that."

"Excuse me. You telling me how to do my job again?"

"I'm just trying to save your sorry butt. If you go into that courtroom this morning, you're going to feel like a fool an hour later. Hell, it'll probably even ruin your pitiful career. No prosecutor likes to find out he's made a big fuss and charged the wrong man with a crime."

"You still don't think Kenilworth did it? Amanda, honey, you're living in a dream world."

"Bobby, listen to me, don't do it. Get it postponed. Schedule it for this afternoon. I guarantee if I can't prove what I'm saying by then, I'll butt out, go home to Atlanta, and sing your praises every chance I get."

"I don't know," he said doubtfully. "What the hell am I supposed to tell the prosecutor?"

"Tell him you're waiting for a piece of key evidence. Tell him you've got the mother of all toothaches and you need to see a dentist right away. I don't care. He'll be grateful to you, I swear it. Please, Bobby," she said one last time.

Then, without waiting to hear if he would agree to get that court date postponed, she hung up and jammed the accelerator all the way to the floor.

Given her lack of familiarity with Myrtle Beach streets, she was proud of herself. She made it to the Horry County Police Station in under fifteen minutes, squealing into a visitors parking place in a way that drew stares from half a dozen cops lingering on the front steps. She raced past them, hoping her friendly wave would reassure them that she was there on important police business.

It worked on all but one, who cut himself out of the pack and trailed along behind her, maybe to see if she was about to turn herself in for reckless driving.

Judging from the shouts coming from one corner of the main office and Bobby Claypoole's mottled red complexion, Amanda guessed that he was trying to do as she'd asked. The prosecutor, a middle-aged man in an expensive suit he'd apparently bought twenty pounds ago, clearly wasn't happy about the proposed change in plans.

Just then Bobby caught sight of Amanda and dragged her over to meet the attorney, who was practically apoplectic. The cop who'd followed her inside remained nearby, obviously fascinated by this turn of events. He might have been hooked by the drama of it all. More than likely, though, he was waiting to see who popped a blood vessel first.

"This is Carter Austin," Bobby told Amanda. To the steaming prosecutor, he explained, "This is the woman who claims she has new evidence that will change the way we proceed with the case."

"Evidence? What the hell evidence could she have that you don't? What the devil are you up to?" the attorney snapped, scowling at Amanda. "I ought to have you thrown in jail for obstruction of justice."

"Me?" she responded innocently. "I'm just trying to help.

Look, I know you're anxious to get this resolved, but if I could just have an hour, maybe less, I think I could get this whole thing straightened out and a full confession on your desk. I guarantee it'll save on court costs, to say nothing of saving your reputations."

"How the hell do you intend to pull that off when Kenilworth won't open his mouth?"

She grinned. "I didn't say he did it," she noted for the record. "In fact, that's the point. I don't think he did."

"Oh, hell, we're back to that," Bobby moaned. "Amanda, honey, couldn't you let that go?"

She lost patience. "Do you want to arraign the wrong man or do you want the truth?"

Carter Austin blustered a few more minutes, but he apparently decided the truth would serve them all better in the long run. Or maybe he just envisioned the embarrassing questions if he failed to listen to her. A pack of journalists reporting on his refusal to listen to a critical last-minute bit of evidence that might have cleared Kenilworth probably gave him palpitations.

"How long do you need?" he asked with an air of resignation.

"I told you, an hour tops."

"I'll get over to the courthouse and speak to the judge." He directed a glare at Bobby. "You'd better damn sight show up over there sixty goddamn minutes from now with a suspect in tow."

"Absolutely," Bobby assured him.

When Austin had gone, Claypoole whirled on her. "Do you mind letting me in on the big secret?"

"Not just yet. I want to see a list of things you took from

the victim's house that morning. I'd also like to see the medical report on Margaret's injuries. Then I need to speak with Kenilworth."

Bobby wasted several of her precious minutes grumbling about her orders, but curiosity eventually got the better of him. He handed over the file. "Don't budge with that."

"I wouldn't dream of it. Besides, I have the feeling you're not planning to let me out of your sight."

"Damn straight."

Amanda flipped through the pages until she found the list of personal property taken from the house as evidence. Margaret's purse was listed, along with its contents. No gun was mentioned.

It was the medical report that clinched it for Amanda. The bullet had been a .22-caliber. More than likely, she guessed, from Margaret's own gun. It had entered her body at an angle, clipping her aorta. She must have bled to death within minutes.

But it was the angle that really intrigued Amanda. She looked up at Bobby, who was staring over her shoulder trying to guess what she was looking for.

"Can you get Kenilworth now?"

"You found something, didn't you? What is it?"

"I need to see Kenilworth."

He sighed heavily. "I'm sitting in."

She nodded. He had every right to be there. She had a hunch, though, when they were done, he was going to wish he hadn't been anywhere near that interrogation room.

CHAPTER

Twenty-three

Hamilton Kenilworth didn't look quite so intimidating in his prison garb. For some reason he hadn't been allowed to change into his suit for the arraignment. Or perhaps he'd gotten word that it had been postponed. At any rate, he seemed like a mere shell of the man who'd walked into *Inside Atlanta* seeking Amanda's help only a week or so earlier. The flat emptiness in his eyes practically tore her heart out, particularly since she now believed she knew what had put it there.

"I'm surprised to see you," he said, his voice cool and distant.

Amanda shrugged. "I told you I wasn't going to give up until I discovered the truth."

"I had no idea when I came to you that you would be so persistent." He didn't sound particularly pleased about it, either.

"Yes, you did," she contradicted. "You just didn't expect things to turn out as they have."

A flicker of a smile confirmed her comment. There was still a touch of arrogance about him. She could tell he didn't believe for a second that she'd found out everything. There were moments when she wished to God she hadn't.

"Okay, then, let's talk about the night you went to Margaret's to get Lauren," she began.

"I've been over that again and again, with the police, with you. Nothing's changed," he insisted stubbornly.

"Not entirely," Amanda agreed. She met his gaze, hoping he would feel the compassion his actions had stirred in her, hoping he would stop this futile attempt to interfere with justice. "Shall I tell you what I think happened that night?"

The suggestion drew an immediate reaction. His eyes became more alert, wary. "Really, I don't believe there's any point to this." He glanced at Bobby Claypoole. "Why don't we just get on with the arraignment? Why was it postponed? I told the prosecutor I'd plead guilty, if we could just put an end to this craziness."

"I talked them into postponing it," Amanda said. "You see, a thought occurred to me when I found out that your wife owned a gun, a gun that she always carried in her purse."

An increasingly stoic Kenilworth showed absolutely no emotion except for a slight tic in his cheek. Bobby, however, was clearly taken by surprise. Amanda rather enjoyed seeing that look of astonishment on his face.

Amanda went on, keeping her gaze pinned directly on Kenilworth. "That gun wasn't in her purse when the police took it from the house that morning. I just checked the evidence list. But I did find out from Tommy Ray Baldwin that it was the same caliber as the one used to shoot Margaret. That's in the case file as well."

"So what? Obviously I killed her with her gun. You've just offered the police a scenario to clinch my conviction."

Amanda shook her head. "I don't think so. You see, the angle at which that bullet entered Margaret's body doesn't make sense, not if you were the one who shot her. You would have had to have been flat on your back, shooting up at her."

The tic in his cheek grew more pronounced, but he wasn't giving up so easily.

"Exactly," he said. "She had hit me with something—a vase, I guess. I fell down, then shot her."

The improvisation touched her, made her wish she didn't have to continue to contradict the valiant, self-sacrificing tale he was trying to weave for the police. "How'd you get the gun?" Amanda asked.

"From her purse."

Amanda glanced at Bobby. "Do you remember where the purse was?"

He didn't even have to think about it. "On a table in the foyer."

"And the body?"

"In the living room." His gaze narrowed as understanding struck. "The other fucking side of the living room."

"Exactly."

"We struggled," Kenilworth said with an edge of desperation. "She already had the gun. It fell out of her hand."

"I don't think so," Amanda said. Despite his repeated objections, she relentlessly continued to paint another picture of what had happened that night. "I think Lauren heard you fighting. Maybe she'd heard it a lot. Maybe she was half asleep and wasn't even sure who was in that room. But she was scared for her mother. I think she got the gun out of her mother's purse. It was just the size that would fascinate a child, wasn't it? She probably didn't even realize that it was dangerous."

Kenilworth moaned and put his hands over his face. "Stop. Please. Leave it alone. Let them put me in prison."

Amanda shook her head, tears gathering in her eyes as she insisted on going on. "It's wrong. I know how much you love your daughter. I know how much you loved your wife and wanted her back, even though you knew she no longer wanted you. Going to prison won't change what happened that night. It was an accident, wasn't it?"

Bobby was listening to the exchange with an expression of shock on his face.

Amanda went on, relentlessly painting a picture of the truth. "Lauren probably had no idea what she was doing; maybe she didn't even mean to pull the trigger. She just wanted you to stop fighting. She reacted instinctively. She got the gun that Mommy carried for protection, the gun she'd heard her grandfather say over and over that her Mommy should use if anyone ever threatened her."

Kenilworth sobbed softly. "Dear God, I swear I never wanted it to turn out like this," he whispered as tears flowed down his cheeks unchecked. "It was my fault. I'm still the one who belongs in jail. It happened because Margaret was trying to protect me. She saw that Lauren had the gun, that she was pointing it at me and pleading with me to leave Mommy alone. Leave Mommy alone. Dear God, she just kept saying it, over and over. She was so scared for her mommy, so angry at me."

"What happened then?" Amanda asked.

"Margaret told her to put it down, but she wouldn't. Her

little finger was on the trigger. The gun was wobbling all over the place. She never would have hit me. But Margaret panicked. She lunged for the gun and it went off. It just went off."

He looked helplessly at Bobby Claypoole. "Don't you see? I couldn't let Lauren go through all the questioning. She just wanted to protect her mother."

"And you wanted to protect your daughter," Amanda said gently. "That's why you sent her to stay with your parents, rather than taking her home with you. Your father knew exactly what happened that night, didn't he? That's why he called Jim Harrison, practically told him that you'd done it. You'd decided together that you would take the blame."

"It was the best way," he insisted.

"And that's why you put up a token protest that you weren't guilty, because you knew everyone would be suspicious if you didn't fight the charges." A sudden thought struck her. "You even moved Margaret's rental car to the marina, didn't you?"

"I had some crazy idea I could frame Gil," he admitted. "You were already suspicious about his affair with Margaret. I thought maybe you'd manage to tighten the noose around his neck a little. I even tossed the gun in the water at the marina. It would have served the son-of-a-bitch right, if I'd sent the police straight to it."

"But in the end you couldn't do it."

He shrugged. "Long before I got back to Atlanta, I saw it would never work. That's when my father and I came up with this strategy. I knew it was more important to protect Lauren than it was to get revenge for an affair that didn't mean a damned thing."

Bobby Claypoole had sunk onto a chair. He looked as if he wanted to cry as well. "Sweet Jesus," he murmured. "That poor little girl."

Kenilworth looked spent. "You can't take a seven-year-old child into court. She doesn't even realize what happened. She knows her mommy is dead, but she doesn't understand that she's responsible. You can't put that kind of burden on her," Kenilworth said. "Please. You have to let my case go to court. You have let me take the blame. Hell, I'll give you a full confession. Just, please, don't drag Lauren into this."

Bobby shook his head. "You're a lawyer. You know I can't do that. You can't, either. It would be the end of your career, the end of everything."

"I'm not important. This is about my daughter. Can't you see that? Look, I know the court will protect her. I know they'll probably rule it an accidental shooting, but she doesn't even remember it. I don't want her put through the ordeal, forced to dredge up whatever memories she has managed to suppress of what happened that night. Just let it be."

Bobby seemed at a loss at first, almost as broken up by what had happened as Kenilworth himself. Amanda had a new respect for him as a result.

"I can't let it be," he said finally. "I wish to God I could, but it would be wrong. It'll be okay. We'll have a psychologist talk to her. We'll help her to get over the trauma. I promise you that. Carter will go along. There won't be a trial, just an inquest. We'll just tell the judge what happened. It'll be ruled an accidental death. I'm sure of it."

"All the coddling in the world won't make up for forcing her to remember that she killed her mother."

"And all the lies won't protect her from seeing her father

sent to prison," Amanda reminded him. "She'll have lost you both, if you try to go through with this."

Kenilworth tried one last time. "I could have been on the floor when the gun was fired. It could have happened just like I said."

This time Bobby looked him straight in the eye. "But it didn't, did it?"

Kenilworth struggled to say the lie aloud, fought to make one last-ditch attempt to protect his daughter, then visibly conceded defeat. His shoulders slumped. "No," he admitted. "It didn't."

Amanda put her hand on his. "It's better this way," she told him. "Lauren needs you at home with her, not in a jail cell for a crime you didn't commit. She's just lost her mother. She needs her daddy more than ever."

A sigh of resignation shuddered through him. "I wonder if I will ever be able to make it up to her."

"From what I've seen," Bobby told him, his voice surprisingly gentle, "what a child needs most is love. You've just proved exactly how much you love that little girl. She'll be fine. We'll make this as easy on her as possible." Bobby looked at Amanda. "I owe you one."

"I'll remember that if I ever get a ticket for speeding around here."

Bobby grinned. "I've been meaning to give you something." He reached in his pocket and pulled out a traffic citation. "You really should learn to hit the brakes when you're going over the limit smack in front of half a dozen cops."

She reached for the ticket, but Bobby shook his head. "This one's on me."

CHAPTER

Twenty-four

Donelli and Pete had good news for Amanda when she finally got home around noon the next day. She figured it must be fantastic news for Donelli to have allowed Pete to stay home from school to wait for her.

"Looks like we have ourselves a son," Donelli informed her.

"Already? What kind of miracle workers did you have on our side?" She glanced at Pete, whose expression was absolutely transformed. She'd never realized how fear and pain had always lurked in his eyes, until she saw them free from both. She held out her arms and for the first time, he allowed the hug without even an instant's hesitation.

"What happened? Tell me everything," she said, pulling up a chair to join them at the kitchen table.

"The PI worked like crazy for the past twenty-four hours. He finally traced Pete's mother. She was living alone on welfare and spending most of that on booze. His stepfather split a while back—right after Pete took off, in fact."

Amanda looked at Pete to see how he was taking Donelli's flat recitation of the facts. There was a calm serenity about him that spoke volumes. This was his past, a past he was glad to be rid of. There seemed not to be the slightest flicker of regret in his expression.

"Anyway, when the PI reported in to me and the lawyer, we decided a quick approach would probably resolve the matter. It did. She agreed to relinquish custody, which means the path will be clear for us to adopt him. The paperwork should go through without a hitch."

After the tangled mess she had just helped to unravel in Myrtle Beach, Amanda couldn't help asking Pete, "Do you want to see her before we go through with this?"

He looked horrified by the suggestion. "No way, man. I don't ever want to see her again. Not ever."

"If you ever change your mind, though, it would be okay with us," she told him. "Maybe there will come a time when there are things you'll want to say to her."

"You mean get all this garbage off my chest?" he said in a derisive tone that expressed clearly what he thought of all the psychological probing a counselor might insist on. He shook his head. "I said it all before I left. She and I, there's nothing between us now. I don't even want her name." He looked at Joe. "We ain't talked about it, but when this adoption thing happens, can I be Pete Donelli?"

Joe looked as if he'd been given a priceless gift. "If that's what you want, then absolutely."

For just an instant Pete hesitated, his gaze fixed on Amanda. "Wait a minute. When you guys got married, you kept your name, right?"

"Because I'd been using it all this time professionally," she said.

"So what do I do? I want people to know I'm your kid, too. Does that make me Pete Donelli or Pete Roberts-Donelli?"

She laughed, then sobered because Pete was clearly in a quandary over the right choice. "You can take your pick when we go into court," she suggested. "Which would you like?"

"Roberts-Donelli," he said at once. "With one of those hyphen things. It'll look real classy, don't you think?"

"Very classy," Amanda agreed, her eyes brimming with tears.

So, she thought, this was what it was going to feel like being a parent. Sad, happy, proud, all mixed into one. And scary. With a kid like Pete, a little panic every now and then was almost guaranteed. She glanced at Joe and saw that his eyes were a little misty as well.

"So," Pete said, regarding them both thoughtfully. "How about a baby sister? I think I'd like that a lot."

Amanda looked at her husband and saw the grin on his face. "Did you put him up to that?"

"Me? I would never use Pete to intercede on my behalf."

"So what's the deal?" Pete said. "Am I going to get a sister or not?"

"Let's see how things go with you," Amanda suggested, grinning at him.

"Hey, wait a minute, you're putting too much pressure on me," Pete said. "I'm just a kid. I'll crack under all the responsibility."

"It's not you I'm worried about cracking," Amanda pointed out. "Maybe you'd better just leave this decision up to Joe and me to work out."

"Well, you'd better hurry up. Neither one of you guys is getting any younger."

"Thank you for pointing that out," Amanda said. "I'll try

to give up my afternoon nap so the three of us can go out for lunch and celebrate."

Pete's gaze narrowed. "Are you being sarcastic or something?"

"She is," Donelli confirmed. "Get used to it."

Amanda allowed herself a full-fledged smile. It was so nice to have a family that understood her so well.

The tragic case was finally over.

Bobby Claypoole was as good as his word. He managed to get Carter Austin on his side and the two presented a united front in court to have Lauren charged with accidentally killing her mother. The judge admonished Hamilton Kenilworth for his part in attempting a cover-up, but no charges were filed against him.

Because of Lauren's age, the charges against her were sealed, which presented Amanda with a major dilemma. How the hell was she supposed to report what really happened in the Kenilworth murder, if Lauren's role in the final outcome was protected by court order?

Though Amanda, better than anyone, knew all of the facts, she couldn't bring herself to use them. Maybe it wouldn't really matter now, but later, when Lauren was grown, what would the impact be if someone dragged out an old *Inside Atlanta* clipping that implicated her in her mother's murder?

Amanda had already made her decision by the time she wandered into Oscar's office on the morning of her deadline. He was going to pitch a royal fit about having to fill all that editorial space at the last minute, but she wouldn't have been able to live with herself if she'd written the story. Let the daily newspapers add to the Kenilworths' grief. She couldn't bring herself to do it.

"Oscar, we need to talk," she said, closing the door so that most of his anticipated explosion would be muffled from the newsroom.

He glanced up from his computer screen. "I've already taken care of it," he said.

"Taken care of what?"

"The story. Soon as you called in and said what happened I killed it. We've got this great little Thanksgiving feature." His expression dared her to make some snide remark. "You know, recipes, decorations, the whole nine yards. Came in from a freelancer just the other day. It'll be terrific."

She refused to be provoked. In fact, Oscar continued to amaze her. She grinned at him. "Thank you."

"For what?" he said with a dismissive wave. "For knowing you'd decide to do the right thing?"

"How did you know?"

"You've got killer instincts when it comes to the bad guys, Amanda, but you're a real soft touch otherwise. There were no bad guys this time. Just victims."

"Yes," she said quietly, thinking of the last time she'd seen Lauren and Hamilton Kenilworth. That cold, austere man had been sitting all scrunched up at a table meant for toddlers, sipping make-believe tea from a doll-sized china cup, while Lauren had chattered away a mile a minute. They were home again. Together.

"This time, thank God, the victims are going to be okay."

Watch for the next

Amanda Roberts mystery

WHITE
LIGHTNING

Coming from
WARNER BOOKS
in October, 1995.

Chapter One

There was no one who could turn a simple request into a command quite like Miss Martha Wellington. Even in her bemused state of mind after being awakened by the phone at 5:15 A.M., Amanda recognized that imperious tone. Less familiar was the weak, quavery fragility behind it.

"Miss Martha, are you okay?"

"No, I am not okay," the grande dame of Georgia society snapped impatiently. "Do you think I make it a habit of calling people in the middle of the night because I feel like chatting?"

Amanda flinched. "Of course not. Obviously, you're upset about something. What's wrong?"

"I'm dying, that's what's wrong."

Oddly, Amanda found she was alarmed less by the bluntly

spoken news than she was by Miss Martha's flat tone of resignation as she delivered it. Though she was well into her eighties, Miss Martha was a cantankerous, stubborn old woman. She had always struck Amanda as someone who would defy death.

Almost as startling as the news itself and Miss Martha's uncharacteristic accepting attitude was the fact that she had chosen to share her present circumstances with Amanda. The last time they'd met, they hadn't parted on the best of terms. Miss Martha had quietly declared herself disappointed with Amanda's reporting on a story involving Georgia's senior senator. Though she normally considered herself immune to what others thought of her, Amanda had been stung by the disapproval from a woman whose grit and determination she'd come to admire.

None of that seemed important now. All that mattered was doing whatever she could to ease Miss Martha's mind, maybe helping her to get back her fighting spirit.

"What can I do?" Amanda asked at once. "Is your house-keeper away? Do you need someone to take you to the hospital?"

"Della's fussing over me like an old hen. As for the hospital, I've been. More than once, as a matter of fact. With luck, I'll never set foot inside another one. I'm planning to die right here at home in my own bed, but not before I set a few things straight. That's where you come in."

Something in her tone alerted Amanda that Miss Martha wasn't talking about apologizing to her for their recent set-to. Whatever she intended to set straight, as she put it, she obviously figured she needed Amanda's journalistic assistance to pull it off. She had never quite grasped the concept of an independent media.

4

"What can I do?" Amanda asked again, though with considerably more caution than she'd displayed a moment before.

"I'll tell you when you get here. Della will have a pot of tea ready and one of those coffee cakes you love so much. Bring your tape recorder. I want you to get every word of this down, in case I don't live long enough to see it through."

Amanda's first instinct was to balk at being summoned like Miss Martha's personal press secretary. It was practically the middle of the night by her standards. Surely this could wait until dawn, at least. Still, her curiosity, always her downfall, was piqued. She'd never get back to sleep anyway. And Donelli was not in his usual spot beside her in bed, which meant she couldn't rely on her husband for diversion.

"I'll be there as quickly as I can," she promised, trying to gauge how long it would take her to shower and dress, then scoot all the way over to Gwinnett County. An hour plus, unless she skipped a few essentials and defied the speed limit. "Give me forty-five minutes."

Miss Martha sighed. "Thank you, dear. I knew I could count on you."

It was not what she'd said about Amanda a few months earlier. As Amanda hung up the phone, she couldn't decide whether she ought to be relieved to be back in Miss Martha's good graces or not. She had a feeling she wouldn't be able to determine that until after she'd heard exactly what it was the elderly woman wanted from her this time.

On her way out the door fifteen minutes later, Amanda paused just long enough to scribble a note for Donelli. She considered fixing breakfast for their newly adopted son, Pete, but the very thought of bacon and eggs made her stomach turn over. She plucked a box of cereal out of the cabinet instead. She figured the note and the cereal were evidence of

5

her new domestication. As she shot down the driveway, sending up swirls of red dust, she couldn't help wondering, however, exactly how long it would be before she slipped off that particular wagon and proved that she wasn't cut out for marriage and parenthood. Lately she seemed to end each day on a note of surprise, stunned to discover that she'd survived another twenty-four hours without visibly failing in either role.

Fortunately, she didn't have much time to ponder how long she could expect that to continue. The roads were practically deserted and, judging from the official lack of interest in her excessive speed, the local police were changing shifts. That particular combination of factors reduced her traveling time to less than forty minutes. Not bad for a drive that generally—and legally—took twice as long.

Miss Martha's housekeeper was watching for her. Della had the front door opened wide before Amanda could cut the car's engine.

"How is she, Della?" Amanda asked as she rushed up the winding brick walkway to the lovely old house. At the moment, with spring a few months away and winter's grip still firmly on, the grounds seemed more desolate than usual. Or maybe Miss Martha's news had finally begun to sink in, filling her with a hint of dread about what she might find inside.

The elderly black woman shook her head. "Agitated." She scowled at Amanda, as if her mistress's mood were her fault. "She's got no business getting herself all in an uproar this way. If you ask me, she ought to let sleeping dogs lie."

The housekeeper's dire tone carried a warning that Amanda couldn't mistake. "I'll try not to let her get too upset."

" 'Tain't up to you. She's made up her mind about this

and nothing you or anybody else is gonna say is gonna stop her. Lord knows I've talked myself hoarse trying to get through to her." She gestured toward the stairs. "You go on up. She's waiting for you. I'll be bringing the tea in a minute."

Amanda would have killed for a cup of strong coffee in place of that weak tea Miss Martha was so fond of. "I don't suppose . . ." she began.

"She ordered tea, and tea is what you'll have," Della said, then softened. "But if you want to stop by the kitchen on your way out, I'll have a pot of coffee waiting."

"Thanks." Amanda started up the wide, carpeted stairs, which she'd never before climbed. Somehow that took on a depressing significance. She'd never known Miss Martha not to receive her guests in one of the beautifully decorated downstairs rooms. The sound of her gold-handled cane tapping briskly along on the wood floors had always heralded her arrival.

Sighing, she glanced at Della. "Which room?"

"Second door on the right." Della hesitated, then added, "Don't be too alarmed by how frail she looks. The doctors say she could last quite a while yet, if she takes it easy. Not that she pays their instructions any mind. She tossed the last bottle of pills they sent over straight out the window."

Amanda found her steps slowing as she reached the upstairs hall. Miss Martha had always seemed so strong, so indomitable. Amanda wasn't sure she wanted to remember her with her energy sapped out of her and her spirits flagging. Unfortunately, before she could turn tail and run, Miss Martha must have heard her footsteps, because she hollered.

"Amanda? Is that you? I heard your car in the driveway. What's taking you so long?"

Amanda followed the sound of her voice and the fit of

7

coughing the shouting had apparently brought on. She entered a room filled with chintz and sheer white curtains. Miss Martha was propped up against a mountain of pillows in a mahogany four-poster bed. An extra touch of blush was the only thing that kept her skin from looking far too translucent and pale. Her blue-veined hands fluttered against the pale rose comforter in a way that hinted at both nerves and a lack of real strength.

Amanda leaned down and kissed her cheek, then took one of those small, cold hands in her own as she sat in the chair that had been drawn up next to the bed. "You look good," she lied, hoping to cover the distress that swept through her at the sight of her old friend.

Miss Martha waved off the compliment. "Nonsense. I look like a sick old lady, which is exactly what I am. Did you bring your recorder?"

"It's in my purse."

"Well, get it out, girl. There's no time to waste."

For once Amanda took the command in stride and fetched her tape recorder. Before she could turn it on, though, Della appeared with the tea and coffee cake. She spent several minutes fussing over Miss Martha, until the older woman lost patience. "Della, that's enough. Bring me that folder I had you get from the vault."

"Should have left it there, if you ask me," Della muttered under her breath.

"I didn't ask you," Miss Martha said, proving that whatever else might be failing, her hearing was as acute as ever. "Just get it and give it to Miss Roberts. I want to get things started."

With obvious reluctance, Della opened the drawer of the nightstand on the opposite side of the bed and pulled out a

8

manila folder bulging with papers and held closed by a rubber band. She handed it to Amanda, muttered something under her breath again about sleeping dogs, and left the room.

Amanda held the folder gingerly. "Why doesn't she want me to see this?"

"Because she figures I might live another day or two if I don't get myself agitated over the past."

"Maybe she's right."

"What would be the point of lingering? I'm ready to go," she said. "Or I will be once this is taken care of. I've waited too long to do it as it is. If I'd gotten into it years ago, maybe my life would have been different."

Her blue eyes, which Amanda had seen alight with humor and snapping with determination, suddenly turned misty. "Very different," she repeated softly.

"Different how?"

"Less lonely," she said at once, then waved off Amanda's expression of sympathy. "Don't look at me like that. I've had a good life. I've done just about everything I ever wanted to do, seen every place I wanted to see and a few I could have done without. I've done it on my own and I take pride in the fact that I've never relied on anyone for anything. That doesn't mean that I didn't have dreams once."

"What sort of dreams?" Amanda asked, unable to keep the slight catch out of her voice despite Miss Martha's determination to shun any display of sympathy. This nostalgic mood of Miss Martha's, these hints at regrets, were filling Amanda with a terrible sorrow. Pretty soon she'd be shedding the tears Miss Martha was holding determinedly at bay.

The older woman smiled. "You may not be able to believe this, but I was young once. Cut quite a figure, in fact."

"Oh, I can believe that," Amanda replied, instinctively smiling back, even though her sad mood hadn't quite been dispelled.

"I'll bet you didn't know that I was engaged, though, did you?"

"I've heard rumors that there was a love affair that went wrong," Amanda admitted. Few people in Atlanta hadn't heard something about a discreet romance that ended badly. Details had been sadly lacking, but Miss Martha's position in society had guaranteed that hints of such a secret wouldn't die. "I never wanted to pry."

"That must have been very trying for you," Miss Martha countered dryly.

Amanda couldn't help laughing. "As a matter of fact, it just about killed me," she admitted.

"Then I appreciate all the more the fact that you didn't ask. Let this be a lesson to you. Sometimes patience does have its rewards. I want you to know about William Ashford. A lot of it is in those papers you have there, but a lot of it was never reported. No one ever wrote that he was a true Southern gentleman, who suffered greatly when his wife died. No one ever wrote about his tenderness or his charm or his wicked eyes. No one ever talked about the kind of father he was to his boy."

Miss Martha sighed. "And no one ever made the connection that he was the man I loved with all my heart and soul, the man I could never forget. When he was in the darkest hour of his life, I kept silent. More than half a century has gone by, but I will never forgive myself for that. I should have stood by him, no matter what."

She turned a steady, determined gaze on Amanda. "I intend to make up for that now, with your help."

As the implications sank in, Amanda's mouth gaped. "You want to make up for something that happened over fifty years ago?"

"I want to prove that something didn't happen over fifty years ago," Miss Martha corrected. "Leastways, not the way they said it did."

"I don't understand."

"You will when you've read through all the clippings in that file."

Given the thickness of the folder, that struck Amanda as a daunting task, and she wasn't at all sure how much time Miss Martha had left. "Maybe you'd better summarize it for me. We'll get everything you remember on tape first and then I can go from there."

"In case I die," Miss Martha said succinctly.

"No," Amanda said just as firmly. "So I'll understand your version before I start digging into all this research you say is filled with lies."

Amanda wasn't sure what she intended to do with any of it. At the moment, she was merely placating a friend, maybe satisfying her own curiosity. If this was something Miss Martha needed to get off her chest, then Amanda could at least do her the courtesy of listening. After that, well, quite likely there was no story, not after all this time.

Miss Martha hesitated, then drew in a deep breath. "William was a bootlegger," she said at last. "There was never any question about that. As for the rest of it, it was all lies."

Then before Amanda could snap her mouth shut and hide her astonishment, Miss Martha added, "They said he killed the revenuer who tried to shut him down."

If Miss Martha had declared that she had once been a stripper in a Paris nightclub, Amanda couldn't have been any more stunned. That she'd been in love with a bootlegger accused of murder certainly was enough to capture Amanda's full attention.

Unfortunately, though, the trail was cold. Amanda couldn't imagine how she could help.

"It's been such a long time," she said carefully. "Witnesses will be dead or their memories will have faded. I really don't see how I can be much help."

"Just because it's not easy? Since when did you walk away from a challenge?" Miss Martha demanded.

"But—"

Miss Martha impatiently waved off her protest. "Besides, you're wrong about everything being so far in the past. When you look in that file, you'll see that history seems to be repeating itself. There was an IRS agent killed less than a week ago during a raid."

Amanda resisted the urge to say *so what*. "And you think there's a connection?" she said skeptically.

"I know there's a connection. It's plain as day. The raid took place on William's property." She looked Amanda straight in the eye. "The man they arrested in this murder is William's grandson. I don't believe for a minute he's one bit guiltier than his granddaddy was. Making and selling moonshine may be against the law—"

"Even now?" Amanda asked. She was astonished. Despite herself, she was growing more and more intrigued. "I thought all of that ended with the end of Prohibition."

"Georgia still has local option laws," Miss Martha replied. "Have you ever tried to buy a beer on Sunday around here?"

"So people make white lightning to get around the laws."

"Exactly. It's a crime, all right, but it's not the same as murder, is it?"

Trying to convince Amanda seemed to have cost Miss Martha the last of her energy. Before Amanda could ask a single one of the hundreds of questions suddenly reeling through her mind, Miss Martha drifted off to sleep. She looked at peace, as if a great burden had been lifted.

Unfortunately, that burden had been transferred to Amanda's shoulders. Miss Martha didn't expect much, Amanda thought irritably. She just wanted Amanda to link a fifty-year-old crime to a recent murder and solve the two of them. Worse, she expected her to do it with one hell of a deadline staring her in the face.

By the year 2000, 2 out of 3 Americans could be illiterate.

It's true.

Today, 75 million adults... about one American in three, can't read adequately. And by the year 2000, U.S. News & World Report envisions an America with a literacy rate of only 30%.

Before that America comes to be, you can stop it... by joining the fight against illiteracy today.

Call the Coalition for Literacy at toll-free **1-800-228-8813** and volunteer.

Volunteer Against Illiteracy. The only degree you need is a degree of caring.

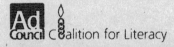

Ad Council Coalition for Literacy